UNHEARD

SENSELESS | BOOK ONE

USA TODAY BESTSELLING AUTHOR

BRYNN FORD

Unheard (Senseless, Book 1)
Copyright © 2022 Brynn Ford
Published by Brynn Ford

<u>More from the Author</u>
www.brynnford.com
brynnfordauthor@gmail.com

CONTENT WARNING

This is a dark romance series involving triggering elements which may be upsetting for some readers. A complete list of tropes and triggers can be found on the author's website.

www.brynnford.com/triggers

SERIES NOTE

Senseless is a series of novellas set in the same world. The novellas are interconnected standalone dark romance stories, and each book follows a different couple. They can be read in any order.

For all the women who fantasize about a hot
stranger in a mask breaking into your house, tying
you up, throwing you in his trunk, and kidnapping
you before inexplicably falling in love with you...

...girl, same.

CHAPTER ONE
Birdie

THE MEMORY OF her death claws at my mind, scratching at the synapses that fire painfully in my brain. I close my eyes and remind myself that this will all be over tomorrow—it will all just be a nightmare I can start to put behind me.

The prosecutor promised that my testimony will put him away for good.

But what if he's wrong?

He could be wrong…

Tears burn behind my closed eyes as the grief over losing Nikki hits me all over again. She's been gone for six months, and it doesn't hurt any less now than it did then. I don't think it will ever stop hurting, but I can't lose myself to grief now. I have to stay alert. I have to stay aware and focused.

One more night.

Testify.

Put him away.

Then, I can grieve.

I swallow the lump in my throat, draw in a steadying breath, pull back my shoulders, and lift my chin. I pace across the soft beige carpet in my living room to stand in front of the mirror hung on the wall above the entryway table. I swipe a finger beneath each eye to pull the tears away.

My shoulders drop heavily as I blow out a breath. "I look like hell." I laugh to myself because that's the understatement of the century.

I tuck a strand of my short ash-blonde hair behind my ear, but a sudden *thud* from somewhere behind me startles me, and my shoulders jerk. I whirl around on a gasp, then freeze as my eyes strain to take in every inch of my living room.

Every light in my humble little house is on—I don't want a single shadow or dark corner for one of them to hide in. With one night to go before the trial, there's no telling what lengths the Senseless will go to silence me and keep their drug ring operational.

Everyone in the entire tri-state area knows that I'm the first person who's ever been willing to stand witness against them… and bets against my life are being made.

Benji Baker wants me dead.

I saw the Grave Digger himself—something few people could claim—and I watched as he killed Nikki. Benji goddamn Baker lured my best friend into his world, and when I tried to save her from losing herself to a life of drugs and crime, he sliced a line across her throat with a knife.

She was standing right in front of me.

I remember the way the crimson saturated the line he drew, spilling thickly from the widening gap. Her bright eyes widened as she stared at me in shock, horror and fear washing the jade away and fading into a muddy olive-green as moments passed, and the life drained from her.

I didn't get to her fast enough to catch her before she fell to the ground. I was struck by fear. I hadn't known Benji from a hole in the ground until that moment, but God help me, I will never forget that man now.

The twisted smile he wore still haunts my nightmares. It was sickening the way his lips curled over his sharp cheekbones, framed by his shaggy, dark blond hair—and those nasty brown eyes that showed his absolute glee for the power he holds over anyone who crosses him.

And tomorrow I'm going to face him in court, tell the judge and jury what I witnessed, get justice for Nikki, and put him away for life. The prosecutor promised that my witness testimony will put Benji away, and I'll never have to fear him again.

But I can't shake the nagging feeling that he's wrong.

How could he possibly be right?

I have to survive the night and make it to court tomorrow before I can find out.

Testifying is dangerous, and I know it. But it's this, and fear tonight, hoping for the best tomorrow, or live in fear daily that he might come looking for me anyway, try to kill me, try to ruin me like he ruined Nikki.

I have to choose justice for Nikki.

All my senses are firing on high alert tonight. My eyes flicker to take in every familiar sight in my living room, making sure nothing looks out of the ordinary. My ears strain to hear the *thud* again—to hear any other sound that shouldn't be heard. My skin prickles with unease, goosebumps brushing across my skin.

I take a single, slow step, moving sideways toward the picture window at the front of my house. I rented this place because that very window let brilliant light shine in—light which warmed the living room and made me feel safe and comfortable. But now it only brings apprehension—so much glass makes watching me too easy.

The curtains are drawn shut, but fear that I'm being watched still grips me. Pressing my back to the wall beside the window, I slip the tip of my index finger behind the fabric, tugging back undetectably, just enough that I can peek outside.

I spot the nondescript, dark green sedan parked at the curb across the street—my police detail. A dash of relief cools the heat of anxiety rushing through me, though it doesn't douse the flame. Officer Hamilton is there—I can see his head bob from where he sits in the driver's seat. Yet knowing he's out there, supposedly watching over me, doesn't make me feel all that safe.

If the Senseless want to take my life, they will. A single

police officer won't do anything to stop them.

A slight creaking sound from the kitchen makes me whip my head around. My heart stalls, panic wrapping around the organ, squeezing until it stops.

Did I imagine the sound?

I'm frozen.

I can't move.

But I can't just stand here and wait.

Waiting is amplifying the rising panic inside me, and I won't be able to get through the night this way.

Slowly, I take a step, and it takes all my bravery to keep my feet moving. I creep over the carpet in my sneakers—which won't leave my feet tonight because I need to be ready to run. I pass the couch and stop in the doorway to the kitchen, halting before the carpet changes over to cheap vinyl. I lean forward, stretching my neck to peek past the threshold.

I breathe a small sigh of relief to find the kitchen empty under the stark fluorescent lighting, but I'm not fully satisfied with my safety yet. I step past the threshold to take in the full sight of the kitchen, scanning across every cabinet, every corner, beneath the table.

I glance over to the door beside the stove—it leads to the small back entryway, which goes out to the carport through an outer door. I look down at the knob, noting the lock is turned parallel to the floor—locked, as it should be.

When I've decided there is no real threat here, I turn

and walk across the living room to the picture window, hooking the curtain with my finger and pulling it back enough for me to peek through.

Officer Hamilton's car is still there…

But where is Officer Hamilton?

I don't see him in the driver's seat. And though a small piece of my logical brain tells me that he must be doing rounds—that he must be circling the house like he said he would from time to time to ensure my safety—my fear tells me otherwise.

A twinge in my gut tells me this isn't right.

Something's not right.

Adrenaline floods my veins, and the rush of it makes me move. With a sudden jolt of fear that startles me like a touch of static electricity, I run around the couch, down the short hall, and sprint into my bedroom. I grab the white wooden door and slam it shut, turning the flimsy lock on the knob.

I turn, suddenly breathless, and press my back against the door, using my weight to hold it shut. For a moment, I feel safe inside my bedroom.

But only for a moment.

Oh, God.

My eyes drop to the carpet beside my dresser and spot the yellow canary figurine lying there. It had been on top of the dresser.

That would've been the *thud* I heard before.

No.

My moment of relief turns to instant fear as movement at the closet door draws my eyes. I'm a deer in headlights as my eyes widen, watching it creep open. Each inch the door widens pushes away an inch of my hope.

Run!

I turn and tug at the knob, but the door doesn't open, because I locked it.

Fuck!

I tug furiously, wasting precious seconds before I realize it. And just as I reach down to twist the lock, the moment my fingertips brush across it, a black leather gloved-hand reaches out, slamming a palm to the door beside my face.

I scream and jump back, but I only run into the hard frame of a tall man behind me. His body slams forward to stop me, pressing me against the door, but I don't let him hold me there. I won't let it end like this.

This can't be how it ends.

I reach out and wrap my hand around his wrist where his hand keeps the door held shut. I grip the black fabric of his long-sleeve, and pull down on his arm with all my might.

He doesn't even budge.

Instead, he moves his arm, slipping it between me and the door, sliding it over my chest. In a flash, his grip rises and his palm encircles my throat.

"No!" I shout before his fingers close around my neck.

He pulls me backward as he squeezes, bruising my tender flesh.

I buck against him, and he changes direction, pushing me forward, pinning me between him and the door. His hand leaves my throat for just a moment to grip my shoulders, and he spins me around to face him instead.

I try to shove him backward, but he slams me harshly to the door. My head whips back and knocks against the wood, my lips parting to let out a surprised gasp as air rushes from my lungs.

I'm not given the opportunity to catch my breath.

He grabs my throat again, crushing painfully, his hand forcing my head to press back against the door with my chin tilted upward. I look up to see a man wearing a white plastic mask which covers his face entirely, except for the eye holes—and I refuse to meet his eyes. The black hood of his sweatshirt is pulled up over his head.

I feel the tug of my eyelids as they widen with fear. Air doesn't flow into my lungs as my body jerks and twists, fighting the unfightable masked man.

He chokes the life from me, second by second, moment by moment, draining what's left of me.

This can't be how it ends…

I gasp without air to suck in. I choke around his grip. My mind fogs over and my vision blackens around the edges.

But through it all, I don't stop fighting.

I won't stop fighting until he takes my last punch, my

last kick, my last hit… my last breath.
I fight, though I know he might just take it all.

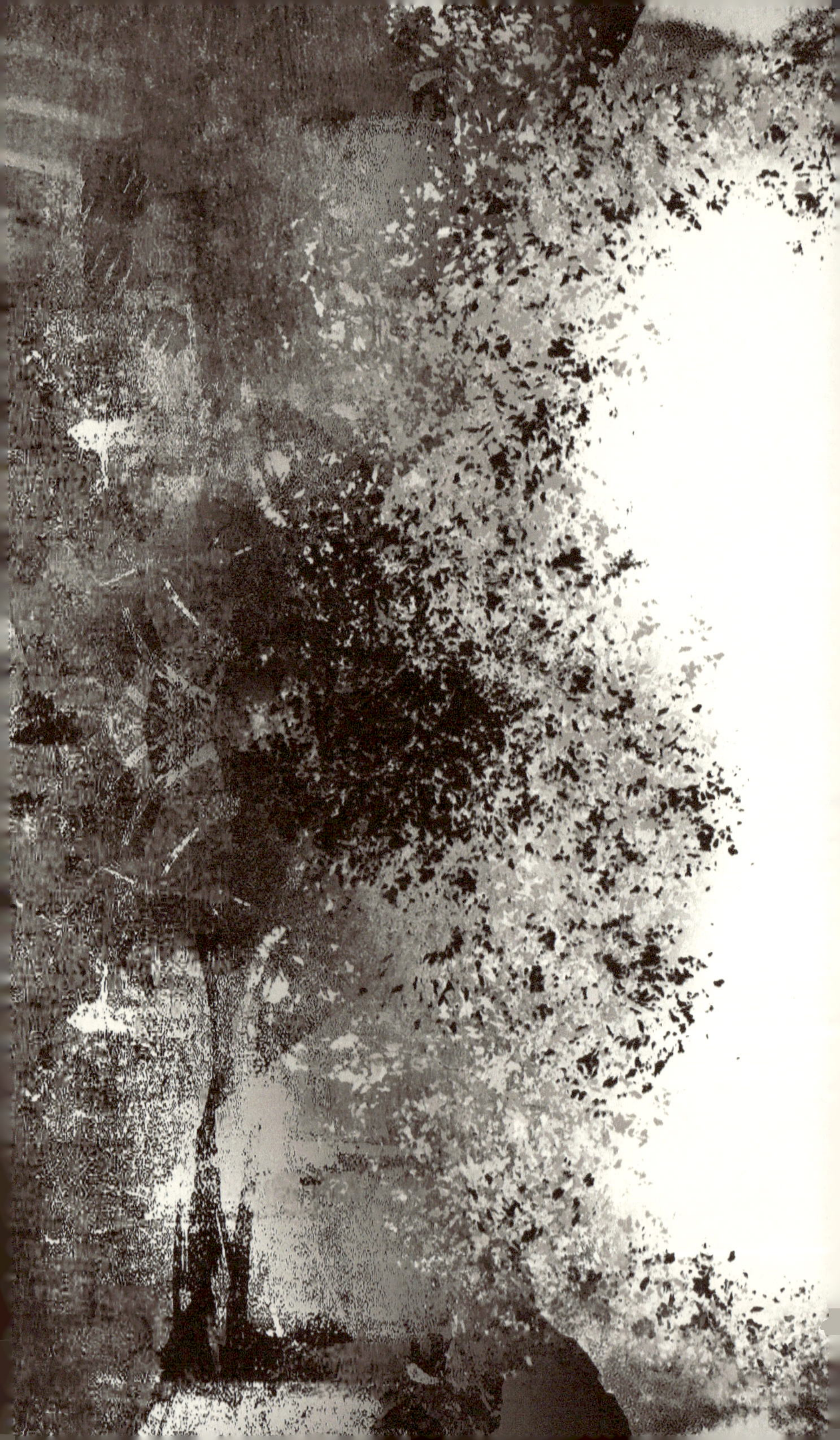

CHAPTER TWO

Birdie

I SLIP TOWARD unconsciousness, but adrenaline roars through my veins, giving me one last bump of energy to fight before I fade away.

My foot connects with his shin. I thrust my arm forward, punching my fist into his gut. It doesn't knock him off me, but his body startles at the impact and it makes him falter.

It's enough.

His grip on my throat loosens, and I draw in a quick breath, the air filling my lungs and granting me a moment's worth of power and fierce determination.

I let the breath cleanse my senses, wash over me, douse me with resolve to get out of this alive.

I will not die like this.

I will not die tonight.

I shove my hands against his chest and push with all my might, throwing my body forward with a quick, forceful thrust which nudges him backward.

My resolve gives me strength, emboldens me, makes me lift my eyes to meet his through the mask. And when they meet, something electric shoots through me, striking me in the gut like instinct—like déjà vu, like suddenly remembering something you didn't know you forgot.

It doesn't make any sense.

I blink, balling my hands into fists at my sides. I'm ready to stand my ground and fight… but so is he. My gaze quickly drops to his wrist as it flicks and a switchblade flips open.

I can't defend myself against a slashing, stabbing blade.

I have to get out of here.

With a swiftness and clarity I was lacking before, I turn, flip the lock on the door, fling it open, and run. I sprint down the hallway, straight through the living room, and skid into the kitchen.

I was determined to keep this house full of light tonight, but the threat has already made itself known. I make the quick decision to flip off the light as I dart into the kitchen with some hope that, at the very least, he may stumble over a chair and it will slow his pursuit.

I dart past the small round table in the center of the small space. I grab the doorknob on the back door—remembering to unlock it this time—and fling it open, crossing into the mudroom behind it. I think about turning left and running out into the driveway, hoping Officer Hamilton is out there.

But what if he's not there?

What if there's another man outside?

What if the man behind me is a decoy, and they're out there, just waiting for me to leave the house?

The Senseless are known for putting those who've crossed them on display in brutal ways—it's not unreasonable to think there might be more of them out there, waiting to do the worst to me.

And though I know escape is necessary, fear of the unknown, of what might be waiting outside, nudges me to the right—down the steps into the pitch-black basement.

The steps creak beneath my feet as I run, the soles of my shoes slapping against the wood with each quick step, echoing through the narrow stairwell.

I land on concrete at the bottom, and the toe of my shoe catches over something in the dark. I trip, but thankfully I don't fall. I stumble and right myself, catching my weight through my forward steps... and then I slam to a stop.

I can't see a damn thing.

I don't ever come down here.

I don't know which way to turn or where to hide.

Why did I run down the stairs?

So stupid!

I hesitate, my chest heaving to catch a breath after being strangled, then sprinting through my house. When I hear the top step creak, I slap my hand over my mouth.

Another creak and I whirl around.

Again, and I step backward.

I back away from the staircase, moving as slowly as the man sent to kill me creeps, one menacing creak after the other.

My heel collides with a box and I side-step to get around it, still backing away until I hit a concrete wall.

I should've run out the door.

What the hell was I thinking?

I'm trapped. There's nowhere for me to run, and I can only hide for so long.

I can't hide forever.

No one can hide from the Senseless.

I expect to hear him call my name as I slump to the floor, then slowly drag my knees back to hug them to my chest. I expect him to taunt me as I lower my face between my knees.

Maybe I should just give up, give in. Maybe fighting is hopeless. I was stupid to agree to testify against a kingpin running the largest growing drug operation through Pittsburgh and the surrounding tri-state area.

But Nikki would've done it for me.

She would've said it was stupidly brave, and she would've been proud of me… She would've been proud, and I can't fucking let her down. I *have* to survive and make it to court tomorrow.

I lift my head, looking out into the darkness. My breaths are rapid and shallow, but I will overcome my fear. I have to overcome it for her. I have to fight this man—I'll kill him if I have to. I'm going to testify tomorrow if it's the last thing I do.

As if my willpower calls to him, I feel the masked man approach me. His presence is like a heavy cloak being dragged through the dark, threatening to wrap around me and smother me beneath its dense fabric; a cloak that catches the stale, damp air and pushes it against me as it floats toward me.

My breath catches as that stale air punches my chest, and a strange thrill ripples from my pounding heart. The high of adrenaline, the buzz of electricity as it spikes my energy once more for the fight ahead.

"Birdie Collins," the man whispers my name, and it creeps through my pores, crawls up my arms, drawing goosebumps in their wake.

The way he says my name sounds like a broken promise. It's a hesitant threat that wraps around my heart, clutches it in a firm grip, and wrings out urgency that drips through my veins.

Get up.

Go after him.

Fight.

Do it for Nikki.

I launch myself from the ground, rushing forward until I collide with a solid chest. I slam my palms against him and shove him back with all my might, but the uncertainty I thought I heard in his voice slips away.

His strong hands close around my biceps, but I push him hard enough that he stumbles while taking a step backward. His grip on me tightens as he falls back, taking me to the ground with him. I land on top of him, the impact against the concrete knocking the air from both of us.

I try to push myself up and off him, but his arms close around me. As he starts to roll, I brace myself, every muscle in my body tensing and tightening against the anticipation of being stabbed.

And that's when I realize that both of his hands are free—he's not holding the switchblade anymore.

Fear quivers through me at the thought of him choking me again—he must intend to strangle me to death if he's put his blade away. As quickly as I can, I wriggle my arms between us to protect my neck. I bring my elbows up and wedge my forearms between our chests as he comes down on top of me.

"No!" I shout into the darkness.

I can't see him, but I can feel him, the weight of him on top of me as I twist and fight. I feel the vibration rumble in his chest as he groans through our struggle—it reminds me that whoever this man is, he's just as human as I am.

It makes me hesitate. He takes advantage, rearing back, wrapping his glove-covered hands around my wrists. He wrestles my arms away and slams them to the ground on either side of my head, my wrist bones crushing into the cold, hard concrete.

I let out a harsh groan… and then he lets go.

But before I can think of what to do with my free hands, his come down on me, latching around my throat and squeezing.

"No," the word is strangled, rasping out of my throat.

I thrash my legs as he leans over his hand, pressing down on my neck, which suddenly feels so small, so fragile. My feet skid and skip across the concrete as breath leaves me for the second time tonight.

I strain to see him in the dark, some strange pull demanding that I see his eyes, that I see the face of my murderer before I fade away.

And as if the universe wants to grant me one last wish before I die, the basement lights come on with a snap, bathing my dank surroundings in light.

"Birdie!" I recognize Officer Hamilton's voice at the top of the stairs.

But strangely, instead of relief, I feel…

I don't know what I feel.

When the man on top of me freezes like a statue, the only thing I want to do is see his face, and I can't fathom why or how I want that… but I do.

My hand snaps forward, my fingers slip beneath the bottom of his mask, yanking it up over his face, knocking his hood back as I push it over his head. It all comes off too easily—as if it was never meant to be there at all—and I see my attacker.

His eyes are dark, a shade of brown so deep, they're nearly black, and his shaggy hair is the same shade. His thick eyebrows draw straight lines over his eyes, which look as fearful as I feel.

His skin is darker than mine, a beautiful shade of bronze that shines with contrast against my ivory tone. He has a beauty mark on his left cheek, just above the scruff of his black stubble, and a few dark spots speckle his skin along his hairline, drawing attention to his strong jaw.

The imperfection of his face is somehow jarring to me—not because it's imperfect, but because his features are beautiful… soft and beautiful.

My killer can't be beautiful.

My killer should be ugly—ugly on the outside to match the ugly on the inside.

And I shouldn't see warmth in his eyes. I shouldn't see anything but hate and sickness and indeterminate rage.

How can I see him as a man?

A creak on the steps turns both our heads in that direction. But his attention returns to me before I remember what's happening. He reaches behind him, and as I turn back to look at him, there's a horrifying *click* as he pulls the hammer back on a gun that must have been tucked inside his waistband.

Sitting back on his heels, his outstretched arms aim the barrel of the gun at the center of my forehead… and all my hope rushes out of me in a single breath.

CHAPTER THREE
Birdie

HIS EYES HARDEN like steel as the metal of his gun taps my forehead, but I can't even flinch for the fear I feel. Every inch of me is frozen in time as I wait for the inevitable.

Will I feel it?

Will it hurt?

Is there life after death?

The terror ripples through me, threatening to make me tremble. I'm about to lose control of myself entirely. But then the steps creak with heavy footfalls padding down them in rapid succession.

The gun leaves my temple.

His arm swings out to the side and my eyes follow his outstretched hand, my gaze fixed on the black weapon.

Officer Hamilton steps onto the concrete, but an explosion rings out and startles me, making every cell jolt and shake me as thick, warm liquid splashes across my cheek. My eyes pinch shut and a shiver runs up my spine. I force them to open and immediately wish I hadn't.

Officer Hamilton is dead on the floor.

I hardly have time to process what happened before the man sinks his fingers into my hair, tangling and twisting the strands as he wrenches me from the floor. My hands shoot up to wrap around his wrists as I scream, trying to pull his hands away, but his grip is fierce. My feet kick along the ground as he pulls me upright, my sneakers slipping in the blood of the only man who could've saved me.

He's dead.

Soon I'll be dead, too.

Why am I still alive?

I scramble to right my footing as my shoes slip over the wet concrete, but no matter how much I twist and turn and fight, I can't shake myself from the intensity of his grip.

He stalks forward toward the stairs, dragging me backward, my scalp aching at the way he pulls my hair. I hear his boot slam onto the creaking steps. Each step *thuds* in time with my backside bouncing against the steps as he drags me.

Where is he taking me?

Why am I still alive?

"Let me go!" I scream.

He doesn't hear me.

He doesn't care.

He should have killed me by now, but instead, the officer is dead while I'm still alive. Dread fills my lungs, filling the empty space and leaving no room for air. I choke on the fear, on the horror of this nightmare that I'm living.

And for what?

All because they killed my best friend.

All because they killed her, and I refused to remain silent.

My heel slams against the edge of the top step as he moves onto the landing, and the jarring motion shakes tears loose from my eyes. A sob breaks free from my dread-filled lungs and the sound of my own sorrow fills the space. But the sound is quickly drawn out into the night as he pushes the outside door open with one hand.

He finally lets go of my hair, and unbalanced, I start to fall. As I slip, and my butt aims for the ground, he catches me, wrapping his arms around my waist and tugging me against his side.

But I fight him.

I put my hands on his elbows and push down. I kick at his shins. I twist and scream, but he's tall and strong, and I don't stand a fucking chance.

He releases me with one arm, strong enough to keep a firm grip on me with the other, and slaps his hand over my mouth—his leather-covered palm is so large that it covers my mouth and nose easily.

I inhale, breathing in the scent of leather. I scream through his palm, but the leather muffles my sound. Violently, he turns me, shoving me back, and my head thumps against the wall behind me.

He looms over me, tall and dark and achingly beautiful despite all the ugliness inside him.

His eyes are warm as he stares down at me, and I hate it. I hate that he looks human. I hate that his stare burrows deep inside me, twists through my gut, and makes me wonder who he was before he became a killer—before he became *my* killer.

He presses forward against me, his elbow jutted out to the side as his hand twists to keep my mouth covered. My eyes widen as I struggle for breath for the third goddamn time tonight. Our eyes are locked as he takes my breath away with his hand over my nose and mouth.

Looking up at him, I wonder if he knows Benji personally. I wonder if he's angry with me for deciding to testify against someone he perhaps considers a friend. I wonder this because of how personal this seems to be.

He has a knife.

He has a gun.

He killed Officer Hamilton so easily, without a hint of hesitation, so I can't fathom what's taking him so fucking long to end my life. He could kill me with the slice of a blade or the pull of a trigger. But instead, he chooses to cut off my air supply, and God, it's frightening.

He holds me in place, pressing harder, the back of my skull sore where it grinds against the wall. My jaw aches as my teeth grind, my dry lips twisting against the leather. My nose aches and I fear if he pushes any harder, it might break.

This would all be so much easier if it weren't for the warmth behind his brown eyes, if it weren't for the way he looks at me as if he's doing me a kindness rather than taking my life.

He's taking my life.

He's weakened me in this fight. In such a short time, he's learned to use force with me, to not let his guard down, to keep my airway restricted until no more air can flow through my lungs.

I can't breathe.

My chest tightens and burns.

My voice scratches as it tries to burst from my throat, but without air, the sound only claws at my vocal cords, leaving my throat sore and raw.

He doesn't let up. He doesn't leave room for error this time. His entire body lays against mine, his weight pinning me against the wall.

He's so warm.

It's strange to have that thought burst through the madness of my suffocation. But his warmth is the only thing I can feel aside from the fear of breathlessness, so I cling to it. I focus on it. I let my body go lax as I realize the fight is useless. I grow tired, weary, my eyelids drooping as blackness creeps in around my eyes. I can't breathe, but he's warm and I let it seep inside me.

"Fuck." I think I hear him mutter. "Fuck, I can't."

But it's too late for him to have a change of heart.

I can't breathe.

My consciousness is fading.

And as I slip into death, I think of Nikki and how I failed her...

I lost.

My killer has won.

CHAPTER FOUR
Hendrix

MY PALMS LAND on the curved metal of the open hood at the trunk of my car. The leather of my gloves creaks against the metal as my grip settles, but I hesitate to close the lid. I look down at Birdie Collins—the woman I'm supposed to murder—who lays unconscious in my trunk.

The way I've laid her was a mistake.

She's curled on her side, her knees tucked up toward her chest, and her wrists bound behind her back.

She looks sweet this way, innocent, like a fragile little thing that needs protection. I didn't see her that way when she was fighting me like a woman desperate to live.

I wasn't prepared for this. I only received the order from Merrick a few hours ago. Benji Baker had waited until the last possible moment to make the call, choosing to end the life of the only person who might pose a threat to his regime—not that putting the goddamn Grave Digger in jail would end the Senseless. His people are everywhere, in and out of the prison system, and one tiny little woman with a name like *Birdie* couldn't possibly bring them down.

So why does he care if she's dead?

He waited until the night before his trial to put out a hit on his only witness. It's not surprising, but I sure as fuck didn't expect to be the one called for the job. I'm not a fucking hitman, and this isn't supposed to be my goddamn job.

I have no experience in this. I've killed before, but only out of necessity. Though it's true that anyone is capable of murder, pulling off a hit with only a few hours to prepare is a monumental task.

If I didn't know better, I'd say I was set up to fail. I'd say Merrick got the call from Benji and chose me for the task, knowing I would fuck it up. Because if I fuck up this hit, there's no way to tie it to either of them. I'll get arrested and they can wash their hands of me because my ties to the Senseless are weak. I'm not one of their junkies-turned-dealer. I'm not dependent on that shit they sell.

I only took numb one time, and I'll never do it again. Numb is the perfect name for that shit—it takes away your senses. Some people say it calms them, and maybe that's true for people who feel too much. But I already feel too little, and numb made me feel like I was fucking dead.

I only work for the Senseless because I owe them. Because I borrowed money from one of them that I couldn't pay back. So I owe them a favor in whatever form they ask.

And they've asked me to take the life of Birdie Collins.

But I've fucking failed so far. I strangled her until she passed out, but I couldn't finish the job.

And I *have* to finish this job.

I don't know what's stopping me.

It was surprisingly easy to kill the cop.

Why isn't it just as easy to kill her?

I gaze down at the petite woman, scanning her small frame. The green scarf I pulled from her closet and wrapped around her pale cheeks cuts in at the corners of her lips where it gags her, and tangles through the mess of her ash-blonde hair over which it's tied.

If I didn't owe them, I think I'd take her right back inside her small house, tuck her into her bed, and watch over her while she sleeps.

Fucking hell.

I felt something resembling passion in the way she fought me. And it's been so long since I felt anything at all, but the feeling of her fight radiated through my skin, seeped into my bones, and warmed my flesh.

It felt like everything I was doing was wrong.

It felt like I was fighting the wrong person.

It felt like I was trying to do an impossible job, not because I couldn't or wouldn't kill another person to save myself, but because some invisible current of electricity rippled and sparked between us.

She hit me like a lightning strike in the middle of a bright blue sky—sharp, electric, a streak of light across an already brilliant blue, bright and unexpected, terrifying and awe-inspiring.

She made me feel.

I don't know her and she made me feel.

I shake my head to ward off thoughts of wonder about the stranger I need to kill. I grip the hood and slam it down hard, metal clanging against metal. I glance around to ensure no one's watching, though it wouldn't matter if they were. My actions are protected by the Senseless—at least, until the job is done, then who the fuck knows?

The job should already be done, dumb ass.

Her body should be lying next to the cop's inside her house, and for some reason I can't make sense of, I brought her here—still alive—tied her up, and put her in my trunk.

I don't have a plan. I don't know what I thought I would do with her now that she's in my car. I don't know where I'm taking her, where I'm going, or what I intend to do once I get there… wherever there is. The only choice now is to drive, because I sure as hell can't take her back inside.

I could.

I just don't want to.

I walk around to the driver's side, open the door, and climb in. I pull off my leather gloves and toss them onto the passenger seat beside me. I pull my keys out of my pocket, but just as I'm about to turn the engine over, I hear her…

She's waking up.

There's a muffled scream—her sound is impressive,

given that she's shut in the trunk and has a gag around her mouth. I swallow dryly, an uneasy tightening pulling across my chest.

Shit.

I don't feel anything for anyone—I'm not capable of caring. So I don't understand why the sound of her cry and her desperate scream from the back of my car tears through me like an earthquake—rumbling, rough, and disorienting.

My jaw tenses and my lips twist as my teeth grind together. I force out a heavy breath, steel myself, and start the engine.

I creep slowly down her narrow neighborhood street, which is lined with parked cars at the curb on either side. I'm lucky I don't get caught in this neighborhood. It's working-class, but this area is still one of the nicer ones… though it probably won't be for long. It's only a matter of time before the Senseless destroy the rest of this city with drugs.

Some working parents' kid will get a taste of numb at a party they didn't belong at. They'll get hooked on it, recruited by the Senseless, then sell it to their friends, who will get hooked on it, too.

Some of them will start killing themselves. When you're on something that makes you feel like you're dead, it makes you want to die—one of the nasty side effects of taking too much of a drug that dampens your awareness and sense of reality. They'll be one of the hundreds of headlines across this part of the country.

15-year-old on 'numb' hangs himself in his parents' house.

18-year-old girl shoots her friend before turning the gun on herself.

5 teenage girls leap to their death in suicide pact after taking 'numb'.

But I suppose that's the American story. The ones who sell us the drugs get richer while the rest of us deal with the consequences.

There's nothing I can do about it.

They can't be stopped.

I'll lose my life if I don't take hers first.

I let my foot fall like lead on the gas pedal and speed the fuck out of town.

CHAPTER FIVE

Birdie

MY VOICE IS hoarse by the time the car rolls to a stop. I don't know how long he's been driving—it feels like it's been hours. I'm nearly ready to give up fighting by the time he's pulled off somewhere quiet.

It's unsettling just how quiet it is when he cuts the engine. There's no sound other than the beating of my heart—no voices, no traffic, no noise at all to indicate that I'm anywhere near civilization. It's disturbing that I don't know where I am, that I don't know where he's taken me. I have no idea what I'm up against when he opens this trunk.

Where did he take me to kill me?

How far away from the world are we?

Is there any hope of getting away and finding help?

I twist my wrists for the thousandth time, grinding my bones together, my skin beneath the bindings sore, raw, and painful. The scarf that gags me is soaked in my saliva, soggy between my lips and rubbing the corners of my mouth raw.

I have to remind myself to breathe through my nose

when my instinct is to gasp in as much air as possible to prepare for each new scream.

But I'm tired now. I'm done now.

The screaming didn't do me any good when I could hear noise around us, and now that we're surrounded by silence, I know it's only a waste of breath.

Why the fuck am I still alive?

Why hasn't he killed me yet?

I hear the familiar sound of a car door clicking open, and my wriggling form settles, as still as a statue. I wonder if I imagine hearing his footsteps as he walks along the side of the car, but if the sound is imagined, it's extraordinarily loud. The *plop, plop, plop* of boots landing on pavement echoes around me in the enclosed space.

The fear is still so present within me, but it isn't hard to cope if I let it burn, let it disintegrate and become sparking embers of anger.

I hear a key scraping against its lock. It catches and the latch pops. I inhale deeply, steeling myself with rage against this cowardly man who should have killed me three separate times already.

If I've survived him for this long, I could survive him even longer.

The trunk lifts and reveals him under a single towering light which hovers high above him and shines down like a spotlight. The darkness surrounds him everywhere else. That single spotlight could be as bright as the sun—trapped in that trunk for so long, my eyes had grown used to the dark. His mask is gone, his gloves are gone, and I don't spot any weapons on him. But most bewildering is his expression.

It's an expression I don't understand. His eyes are warm and soft, yet cold and hard at the same time. His jaw is tense, but his mouth is relaxed, plush lips drawing a straight line across his stubbled cheeks.

I push out a heavy breath through my nose, and my anger rushes out with it. It crosses the space between us, touching him before dissipating and scattering into the night.

He tilts his head to the side as he watches me, thick eyebrows drawing together in a 'V' as he looks down at me, and a beat of silence passes where nothing happens.

It's just quiet and dark and *us*.

And for a brief, strange moment, I feel peaceful.

I think it's something about his eyes that does it… not his eyes exactly, but rather the curiosity that plays in the darkness of his gaze.

Is it curiosity for me?

I'm curious about him.

I don't want to be curious about him.

I should feel some sort of shame for having any curiosity about this would-be killer who kidnapped me and stuffed me inside his trunk… but I don't.

And that's what has me quiet and still—not for the absence of fear or anger, but for the presence of some strange, oddly hopeful curiosity.

I want to know what he's thinking as he watches me, bound and trapped in the trunk of his car. I want to know what he thought when his hands were around my throat, choking the air from my lungs. I want to know what he was thinking when he held the gun to my head but couldn't pull the trigger. I want to know why I'm still alive and why I'm still with him.

His arms are stretched with his hands still holding the lid of the trunk, gripping it as if he's only a moment away from slamming it shut again. The thought of being shut in here for any length of time punches painfully through my chest and forces strangled words through the gag in my mouth, but the words are unclear—merely moans and whimpers around the scarf.

"Goddammit," he mutters, twisting his head away, looking over his shoulder into the dark emptiness behind him.

One hand comes down from the lid of the trunk and I jerk away as his fingers reach toward my face. His fingertips are soft, but he scratches my cheek with his jagged nails as he grapples for the scarf. He hooks two fingers beneath the wadded fabric and tugs it out.

The taut material catches on my bottom lip as he pulls it down, but then my lip springs free as the wet fabric slips down my chin. I turn my neck, twisting my head as I strain my jaw to encourage the scarf to slip away from my face.

His touch lingers, his knuckles bent beneath my chin. They drag over my jawline to brush my cheek, the warmth of his stroke heating my cool skin.

It heats my insides, twisting my guts with a strange combination of fear, loneliness, but most inexplicably, need.

I feel need…? What? Why?

I desperately try to rationalize this in my mind.

It's because I don't know where I am.

It's because I'm scared.

It's because he's the only person around to connect with, and I don't want to be alone in this.

It's because he's beautiful.

None of that is rational, I know. I must be out of my goddamn mind from tonight's events for me to feel that horrible, disgusting, pleasant tug of need deep in my core.

I know that it's because of this man that I've stared my own death in the face tonight. I must be in a state of pure lunacy to think I feel anything resembling attraction for this horrible man.

Yet, I can't stop staring at him.

I don't understand where it comes from or if it's even there at all… Maybe I'm only imagining a beautiful face with eyes that threaten to open like windows and show me his very soul.

My gaze traces the line of him and stops at his throat as he swallows hard, his Adam's apple bobbing as he pulls his hand away from my face. Then he reaches with both hands, slipping large palms between my pinned arms and waist.

His hands slide up my body, grazing the sides of my breasts as they move to grip my underarms. I flinch at the intimate touch, a strike of lightning flashing through my insides.

My mind urges me to recoil, but my body—my stupid fucking body—arches into his touch, begging him to grab me and pull me out of this pit.

He lifts me sideways with ease, gradually raising me onto my knees. I let him do that much, but as soon as I'm upright, I jerk and twist my body, trying to free myself from his grip, which is confusing my senses.

"Why haven't you killed me yet?" I demand through gritted teeth, anger tinging my words to mask the confusion coiling my insides.

His grip doesn't loosen with my movement; if anything, his grip has become more insistent. His palms curve, the heels of his hands pressing into the sides of my breasts, his fingertips digging into my back as he draws me forward.

He pulls the top half of my body over and out of the trunk with ease, but my thighs, knees, and shins scrape along the lip as he drags me out. Then my feet drop to the ground heavily the moment he tugs me free.

I know I should run the moment my feet hit the pavement, but I don't… and I don't know why.

Pick up your feet and run.

Run.

Run!

Before my disobedient body can catch up with my mind, he lets me go, and I stumble forward, unbalanced, my body swaying into his. He reaches around me with both hands—lightning fast—and slams the trunk shut, slams his body against mine, slams my ass against the car.

I gasp as his palms slap down on the trunk on either side of my hips as he pins me in place with his body and leans over me. He's so tall, it's like looking up at a mountain this close. He looms and heat builds between us… rippling, searing heat.

When he speaks, my ears perk up with attention, intrigued by the deep, soft, sultry timbre of his voice. "There's only one way out of this for you," he says, "and that way is death."

I grit my teeth. "Then why haven't you killed me yet?"

He takes in a slow, deep breath, and I feel his chest rising against my body, reminding me that he is as alive as I am, as human as I am. Knowing that is what makes me see the contrast of him—it's where I see softness that contradicts hardness. It's where I see a killer, but not a ruthless devil.

But isn't he?

He and I are both human, and in that, we are the same.

"I don't know," he finally says, the words slipping out of him like a breeze. "Maybe I'm taking the wrong approach." His head inclines with a small twist of his lips that looks forced. "Maybe I just need to take my time with it."

He reaches out with his finger, hooking a single strand of my hair and twirling it. It's as if he wants to come off as menacing, but I'm not seeing him that way right now—though I certainly did when I first laid eyes on him wearing that awful mask, popping out of my bedroom closet to put me in my own damn horror movie.

But he's had so many chances to kill me, and he hasn't. I think the novel fear of being chased and attacked is somehow… wearing off?

I'm not terrified like I was before. It's all turned to anger, and his taunting spins the weave of it into golden threads of rage.

I narrow my eyes on him and jerk my shoulders back to straighten, trying to amplify my height, which is meager compared to his. "I'm not afraid of you."

"Could've fooled me with all that screaming."

I lift my chin to meet his dark eyes. "You tried to *murder* me, then when you couldn't, you kidnapped me and drove me around in the trunk of your car! Who wouldn't be screaming?"

"I wouldn't have wasted my time screaming," he says.

His hips subtly shift against mine, and I can feel the thickness hiding behind his jeans. I inhale sharply at the friction, suddenly aware of the tension pulling through my stomach. My head bows as I glance down between us, but then I quickly snap back up again, trying to regain the eye contact we lost.

But I miss.

My eyes land on his lips instead, which are parted, heated breath escaping from between them. He pushes closer, and I feel the full weight of him against me, crushing me to the car.

It's not just his weight that I feel, but his density. I can feel the particles of his soul and how tightly packed together they are. There's no space between them, no way to penetrate and see through him… With him in front of me, I feel heavy in the pull of his gravity, like a lonely moon orbiting a strong planet.

I forget to breathe with my eyes on his mouth and I pull my shoulders back to lift my chest, to try to put some space between us, to remind myself to take a deep breath and let air fill my lungs.

But as I pull back, he leans forward, his finger falling from the strand of my hair, and his palm grazes my cheek instead.

His eyes are fixed on my mouth, and the way he looks at me is unsettling—as if he could eat me whole… as if he wants to devour me. I swallow hard and blink, forcing my eyes to look away because I can't handle the intensity of the way he watches my mouth.

There's nothing but darkness all around us aside from the light overhead—he's brought us to an empty parking lot nestled between a couple of run-down brick buildings that look abandoned.

Fuck. He could do anything to me here and no one would know.

Fear tries to creep back in, but I force anger to flush it out. I narrow my eyes, let my eyebrows slant heavily toward my nose, and open my mouth to tell him off.

And then his lips land on mine.

I'm stunned.

I can't move.

I'm motionless as he forces a kiss I didn't ask for.

I expect roughness; I expect a bruising kiss. I expect his hand to slip behind the back of my head and hold me in place so I can't escape, even if I fight.

But his hand doesn't move from my cheek. It remains gently in place—*gently.* And his kiss is soft, a tender touch of his lips to mine, a caress of skin against skin.

What in the actual fuck is this?

And why the fuck do I like it?

Warmth spreads from this kiss, creeping down my insides, spreading through my belly and tightening my core. My hips shift forward against my will, and in response, his hips push back, pinning me between the back of the car and the growing hardness in his jeans.

Jerking my head back, I gasp. His eyes watch me with curiosity and confusion, as if he hadn't planned to kiss me but was pleased that he did all the same.

I want him to kiss me again.

The moment is gone just as quickly as it came. It snaps

away like the flip of a switch, cutting off the light and bringing us back into darkness. His warm hand falls from my cheek, coming down with the other so he can grip my biceps with both hands. With a sharp step back, he yanks me away from the car, whirls me around to face it, and slams me forward against it.

My hips collide with metal and air is forced out from my stomach with an *oomph* as he shoves me down, folding me onto the top of the closed trunk lid. He folds over me, hips to my ass, hard chest coming down on top of my arms, which are still locked behind my back.

I turn my cheek and it touches cool metal. "Let me up!"

His warm breath kisses my cheek, brushing away the cold. "You're making it very difficult for me to do my job."

"Did it ever occur to you that you might just be really fucking bad at your job?"

"Birdie," he purrs my name as if he knows me and the sound of it sends a shiver down my spine—I like the way it sounds and I don't understand that, "if you were anyone else, the job would've been done in your bedroom."

What does that mean?

My jaw grinds and twists as I try to remain firmly in my rage, but God, the way his body feels against mine is overwhelming my senses.

Hitman.

Killer.

Senseless.

Don't forget who this guy is.

"You could've done your job in the bedroom. You could've done your job in the hall. You could've done your job in the kitchen. On the stairs. In the basement." My voice rises in frustration as I speak. "You have a knife. You have a gun. You could do your job *right now*. Do your goddamn job!" I scream. "Do your fucking job and get it over with!"

He's silent, but the speed of his breathing has increased, the warmth of his breath against my cheek puffing in time with my rising agitation.

His fingers graze my ear as they hook around the strands of my hair, tucking them behind my ear, and turning his face so he can look me in the eye.

"It would be easier if you stopped," he says.

"What?"

"Stop."

"Stop *what*?"

I thrust back, trying to knock him off me, but he has me pinned, and all I can feel is how much closer the arching of my back brings me to his warmth. He groans and I feel it reverberate across my face.

"Stop making me fucking *feel*," he grits.

He falls heavier against my back, shuffles closer so his thighs press harder against the backs of my own… and I think I feel him hard against my ass. He squirms as he moves into me, and now I'm sure of it.

God, why does that make me *feel?*

I thrash, throwing myself back, trying to fight against the sensations creeping beneath my skin. I buck and jerk and twist my body against the metal I'm pressed to. My struggle turns to a fight as he wrestles me for control, as we both grunt and groan and our bodies bump and shift.

I feel a thrill—a strange sense of excitement in the way we seem to move together more than we seem to move apart.

Then suddenly, my bindings break and my arms spring apart, as if he sliced me free with the knife he held earlier.

Is this it?

Is he going to stab me?

Slit my throat?

Jab it into my side?

Even though I think of all the ways he could kill me with that knife, somehow, I know he won't. I don't know how I know—maybe it's all the missed opportunities he's had so far—but I know.

His hands circle my wrists, but I'm desperate to pull my arms free, tired of being bound and held. I pull away, tearing my arms from his grip. I slam my palms on the hood on either side of my head and try to push myself up.

He doesn't stop me from lifting and arching my back. He grabs my waist and a current of unwanted lust ripples from his touch. He spins me around to face him again, and I put my hands up against his chest to push him away—only I don't push.

He keeps me tight against the car, his body smothering mine, and I feel his erection against my stomach.

"Fuck, who *are* you?" he rasps.

I lean back, my mind knowing he's dangerous, though my body hums for this closeness. "Who am *I?*" I try again to bring anger to my features, though I don't know if I'm successful. "Who are *you?* I don't even know your name—"

He bends and kisses me roughly, bruising my lips as his arms snake around me. One large hand slips up my back to cradle my head, fingers combing into my hair as he holds me in place.

I jerk my head back, lift my hand, and slap him across the cheek, a loud *smack* echoing into the empty parking lot.

The echo surrounds us for a moment before fading into the darkness. I watch him with narrowed eyes and parted lips, shocked by the passion he gave me in that kiss—shocked by the way he looks at me as though he *needs* to kiss me again.

Seconds pass, and I feel like I'm trapped with him in a void, a dark space that doesn't exist except for the moments we share within it—and that feeling of disconnection from the world isn't nearly as distressing as I would've expected it to be.

It's freeing.

His grip on my head tightens as his eyes dart to my mouth, as his tongue sneaks out to wet his lips, and draws my attention. He exhales slowly with resignation, and then his mouth is on mine again, lips wet and parted, ready to devour me.

I'm ready for it this time—I think I *want* it this time.

My fingers curl over his chest to grip the fabric of his black hoodie, holding on for my sanity as my lips part to welcome his tongue inside my mouth.

And God, do I welcome it.

His tongue is thick and wet and wild, licking purposefully across mine and hastily drawing me into a sensual dance. I pull him closer, my hands tugging at his hoodie without my conscious thought.

I should be taking him off-guard, shoving him away, fighting, and running for my life.

Yet I draw him closer.

I welcome his kiss.

And when his hips thrust forward, seeking friction against his hardening cock, I thrust back. My legs part, spreading for him as he moves into me, and a liquid rush of warmth sinks between my legs.

His teeth catch my bottom lip and I cry out as he tugs. His fingers curl in my hair, his touch turning rough and forceful, but I'm not afraid of it.

I want it.

I think I need it.

His free hand slips over my hip and down the side of my thigh. His fingers sink into my flesh before he hitches my knee up sharply against his hip. As he pulls my leg, he thrusts, and like a magnet, my hips are drawn to his. My core clenches, begging for friction, for touch, for relief from the man who was sent to kill me.

What the ever-loving fuck is happening?

All the tension and fear and horror of this awful night bubbles to the surface and begs to burst. My hands grip tighter and pull him closer. My tongue swipes across his and a strangled moan claws its way out of my throat as he meets me, lick for lick, with eager desire. He shoves the moan back down my throat with the force of his own, which vibrates through my lips and sinks inside me.

His hand slides up the back of my thigh, fingers curling around my cheek and digging into my flesh as he lifts me, slipping my body up to sit on the trunk. I let go of his hoodie and throw my arms around his neck as he bends over me, deepening our kiss impossibly more.

His body rolls against me and mine sinks toward him, my bottom slipping easily along the metal until we collide. I gasp as the hard bulge between his legs hits my pussy.

Our kiss breaks, but his lips don't leave my skin. He nips along my jaw, painting a trail of lust across my skin. His hands reach around me to grip my ass, pulling me down, pulling me closer, holding me steady as he rolls his hips.

My eyes flutter open to catch him in the glow of the single overhead light, which casts shadows all around us. I blink at the surrounding darkness, and it only confirms that he's taken me away from reality into darkness, into a void where only he and I exist.

And with the perfect roll of his cock grinding into me, my body comes to life.

I lift one hand, sink my fingers into the thick raven strands at the side of his head, and tug. He lifts his head to look at me, and I hold him steady with his nose touching mine, keeping him close as I bring my stare to meet his.

His eyes are hooded and his plump lips are parted, panting through heavy breaths as we watch each other, as I slip and switch the angle of my hips to seek friction where I need it.

A thousand words pass between us as we stare, as we grind, as we chase relief.

Touch me.

Kiss me.

Fuck me.

End me.

My clit throbs as tingling pressure builds from seemingly nowhere. I've never felt so turned-on, so supercharged, so desperate and ready.

And all our clothes are still on.

I hook my legs around him, dig my heels into the backs of his thighs, and use the leverage to change my angle. "Oh," I moan as I find the perfect spot.

He rests his forehead against mine, his eyes still watching me, holding me in his gaze, drawing me into his very soul.

"Birdie…" he breathes my name and both of our chests sink at once as a sated breath escapes us in unison.

We're desperate for relief and satisfied beyond reason all at once.

A shared thought passes between us, and somehow, we both know that we need the release. Rhythmic grinding quickly fades into frenetic dry fucking. My legs tighten around him, his hips jerk and thrust, hard and fast.

"Yes," I encourage, my eyes locked on his as the car rocks beneath us, swaying to the chaotic tempo of our movement.

His eyes dart across my face, taking in the sight of me as if I'm something worthy of laying eyes on. His gaze settles on my lips, and his tongue slips across his. The sight of his hunger tugs a knot tight in my belly. As it tightens, I gasp, arching my back, clinging to him as I tilt my chin to offer my kiss… and he takes it.

With eyes wide open, he kisses me, and my soul opens to devour every dark crumb of this insanity.

There's a pinch, a tingly tightening through my clit, and then a burst of starlight, fire and heat shooting through me as I come unexpectedly through all the layers of clothing.

My fingers curl, fisting the fabric at his back as a tense shudder tears up my spine. His lips break from mine, but he's still in my soul, still sharing my breath and tasting my truth.

"I want you," he mutters as his thrusting loses pace, as he wildly fucks and grinds.

I'm lost for words, lost in his gaze as he stares deeply and sees all of me.

I want him to want me.

I want him to taste me, to have me, to come inside me.

Have I lost my damn mind?

He grunts and his breath catches as he strengthens his grip on my ass cheeks, holding my hips steady for him to grind and thrust.

I don't speak.

I don't move.

I only hold him there between my legs and keep him caught up in my stare.

If there were a good time for me to try to fight him off and run away, this would be it, this moment where he dangles on the edge of ecstasy. I should shove him and run, but I don't think I can do it.

I *know* I can't do it.

I'm too curious for the look on his face when he comes undone.

His lips part and so do mine, panting madly through the desperate tension that holds his expression. He's close. He's fucking me through his jeans, yet he's close.

I don't need to come again to feel the power of the universe between my thighs—the way he so desperately needs me grants pleasure enough to have me begging for his climax.

The man who was meant to end my life tonight is

desperate in my hold—begging, panting, needy for me.

Oh my God.

I let my fingers comb through his hair. "Come..." I pant. "Please."

As I command it, he releases, and it's the most beautiful thing I've ever witnessed. The way he succumbs to it, fighting through it, straining as though he tries to control it makes me feel powerful and proud.

It makes me feel desired, wanted, needed.

I've never really been needed this way before.

The truth of that sinks heavily in my chest as his ragged thrusting smooths to a rolling grind—and our eyes remain locked.

We watch each other as we fight to steal the shared breath between us—though neither of us wins. I blink too long, breaking the connection, and he falters.

His eyebrows fold to a 'V,' his eyes narrowing on me and drawing a quick line across my lips before he rips himself away from the moment. With fury—and I don't know whether it's real or forced—he grabs my wrists and violently jerks my hands away.

My legs instinctively tighten to hold on to him, but his grip is strong as his hands land on my knees and shove, tearing me away from his body. My feet land on the ledge of the bumper and my palms hit the metal on either side of my hips to keep me sitting on the car.

He takes three steps backward in quick succession,

bringing his hands up to run through his dark hair as he looks at me with bewilderment. He pauses to watch me.

I should run.

He tilts his head to the side as he drops his arms heavily against his sides.

Why am I still sitting here?

He charges toward me again with an outstretched hand and fury on his face, and before I can react, his hand latches around my throat.

I didn't even try to get away!

He snarls, his lip twitching to bare his teeth in anger, "You… You're fucking…" He huffs out a heavy breath and his eyes narrow on mine. "You're as good as dead."

CHAPTER SIX
Hendrix

WHAT THE FUCK *is happening?*

I should've killed her four goddamn times by now and instead, I took her to an abandoned warehouse parking lot in the middle of bum-fuck-nowhere and dry humped her against the trunk of my car.

And I fucking came… *She* fucking came.

We both came just from grinding against each other, and I don't know that I've ever felt so painfully, desperately needy in all my life.

She makes me feel, and feeling is frightening—it's overwhelming, draining, exhausting. But it's also intoxicating, maddening; it's a natural high I've never felt before.

Incomparable.

I'm terrified because finding a high like this is dangerous. The way she strikes me like lightning feels so fucking good that I want her to strike me again and again.

I think I need it.

I think one hit of her was all it took to get me hooked, and I feel the pull of addiction creeping around the edges of my mind.

I feel her pulse thrumming beneath my hand where I grip her throat, quick and steady. I want to feel it quicken beneath my touch, and I can get that from inciting fear, but now I know I can get it from explosive pleasure, too.

Shit, this is the kind of intensity I've been lacking in my life. Doing a hit job for the Senseless gave me a pulse of adrenaline, but kissing her, touching her, watching her come made the dam break, causing a fucking flood of it.

Her eyes are wide. She's fearful of me—as she should be—but it's not the same fear I saw before. It's not the same fear you should have for the man who's trying to end your life—which I haven't proven I'm actually capable of doing.

I sense that her fear rests more in the realm of the unknown, much the same as mine. I don't know what just happened, how it just happened, why it felt so good… why it felt so *right*. But as her eyes fall to my lips and her tongue licks across hers, I feel the perfection of her presence threaten to consume me again.

She pulls me toward her without asking, without touching. It's just the gravity of her that makes me move in closer, and I'm trapped inside her orbit.

My fingers squeeze around her throat as I lose myself again, bending to kiss her roughly. She arches her back, her body naturally seeking mine, though she doesn't reach for me. Her palms remain firmly planted on the car beside her hips.

But she doesn't pull away from my kiss.

And more profoundly telling than anything is the fact that she kisses me back—even after the rush of our desperate grinding has passed, she still kisses me back.

I give into it, give into *her*. My thumb sweeps beneath her lip, and I feel the vibration of her groan of approval beneath it.

I can't stop.

I can't let go.

I want her.

It takes all my willpower to end the kiss, and even then, I can't tear myself away fully. My lips remain a whisper away from hers, and I feel her swallow hard beneath my hand. I loosen my grip as I fight to catch my breath, as she fights to catch hers, and I let it slip down toward her collarbone.

"You're not going to hurt me, are you?" Her whispered question comes out as if she already knows the answer and is stating the obvious for my benefit.

"I'm supposed to—"

"You can't."

"I know I can't." Frustration edges my tone as my thumb absently caresses her skin. "I know I fucking can't, and it's gonna cost me my life."

Her breath catches. "Stop touching me… please."

"Why? Because you don't want me or—"

"Because I can't focus." She presses her eyes shut. "Because I can't breathe, I can't *think*..."

I bring my hands up to grip her jawline, tilting my forehead to press against hers. "Because you want me?"

She lets out a slow, heavy breath, her features softening in a way that threatens to gut me. "I came for you..." Her eyes slowly open and catch hold of mine. "That's never happened from just... I never—"

"Came for a stranger with all your clothes on?" I chuckle, and the feeling of such a sound bouncing out of me somehow lightens me.

"Never." One of her hands reaches up to clutch my wrist, fingers curling softly around the fabric of my hoodie sleeve. She doesn't try to pull my arm away, but instead, she holds it there. Her eyes fall shut again. "I should still be afraid of you, shouldn't I?"

"Are you?"

"Yes? I don't even know your name."

"Hendrix." My name slips from my lips in an instant before my mind even takes a moment to consider the disastrous implications of sharing my name with the woman I'm supposed to kill.

I can't do it.

I can't kill this one.

I just fucking can't.

"Hendrix," she repeats, and the way her soft lips curl around my name hits me like a lightning bolt all over again.

"What happens now?"

She could rip me to shreds with the use of my name alone. I want to hear her say it again. I want to hear her whisper it against my ear as I bury myself deep inside her. I want to hear her whimper my name as she begs me to make her come. I want to hear her scream it as I fuck her to ecstasy.

I don't know how to respond to her.

I don't know what to tell her.

I've fucked up everything, and this puts me in deep shit with the Senseless.

But it's like the universe has decided for me—decided for *us*—that death won't find this woman tonight. And if it does… it won't be by my hand. I know that much.

The burner phone in my back pocket rings and my gut sinks. I swallow hard and drop my hands from her face. Stepping back, I regretfully drag myself away from her. Her eyebrows dip inward, watching me with worry as I step backward, slowly pulling the phone from my pocket.

I glance down at the small, archaic call screen, which flashes a number I don't recognize, and that means it's a call from *him*—the Grave Digger himself.

"Fuck," I mutter, spinning away as I stare down at it. I pace away as I run a hand through my hair.

I'm suddenly very aware of the cum on my thigh—the sticky evidence that I've completely lost my grip on reality, lost my control of this situation, and have gotten myself into a mess that's impossible to clean up.

I whirl around and lift my head, almost half-hoping that she's run away, just to give me a reason to chase her. But she's still there, perched on top of my car, heels resting on the bumper and knees still spread for me. She still holds tension through her body, fear for what I'll do—of course, she does.

But I think she and I both know at this point that she can let go of the tension. She can let go of it because I've already tried and failed. I know I'm capable of murder, but the thought of doing it to *her* is something I can no longer fathom.

And I don't fucking know why.

"Don't say a fucking word," I tell her seriously with lifted eyebrows.

She doesn't move or respond and that's acknowledgment enough for me.

I take in a deep breath and answer the call. "Hendrix."

"Is it done?" Benji asks.

"Yes," I say quickly, knowing that if I hesitate, he might sense my lie.

"Really?" I immediately sense the skepticism in his tone. "Where's the body?"

Fuck. How do I answer that?

My eyes flicker to Birdie, and I instantly regret it. Her beauty is distracting, but her scowl is a reminder of what I was supposed to do and how I couldn't. She knows who

I'm talking to, or at least she can guess. And the way her eyes narrow on my phone with disdain makes me curious to know the details of what happened to her and why she's the only witness who ever had a chance of putting the Grave Digger behind bars.

"Where's the body?" Benji asks again.

I swallow. "In the trunk of my car."

"And is that a *dead* body, Hendrix? Or is she still alive?"

"If you're asking me if I did my job—"

"That's exactly what I'm asking. See, I sent my cleanup crew to her house, and all they found was a dead pig in the basement. But you know what they didn't find...? *The fucking witness.*"

"I did my job," I lie.

"So you took her somewhere else to kill her? Because my crew didn't find a trace of anything else in the house aside from signs of a struggle. Unless you're the cleanest killer on the planet, which I highly fucking doubt given the mess you've made of your life, then I have to assume she's *still fucking alive.*"

I hesitate, then finally say, "She's dead."

I hate the thought of that. I hate the thought of her dead, of me killing her... of *anyone* killing her. I rake a hand through my hair.

"Then it shouldn't be any problem for you to bring her to a dump site."

I grit my teeth. "No fucking problem at all."

"Good. I'll have two from my cleanup crew meet you there. I'll text the location. Bring the phone with you, and they'll take care of it when you arrive."

"Fine."

"And if she's not dead when you get there, Hendrix, mark my words… Your life will be fucking over. You'd better not be pulling any of that savior-of-the-fucking-universe shit with that bitch."

Rage drips through my veins and blackens my heart. I do what I have to do to survive, and I don't play savior to anyone, least of all a stranger.

She's not a fucking stranger, though. She's… she's the only sensation I've ever known. She's the creeping, tingling feeling through limbs that have fallen asleep. She's awakening things within me that I've never felt before. Before her, I was senseless and now…

Now I feel it all.

I fucking feel it all and I want more.

Benji doesn't say goodbye, he simply ends the call, and I pull the phone from my ear to glance down at the screen. I wait for a few seconds and watch it until the text comes through, indicating the location of his cleanup crew.

Allegheny National Forest.

A two-hour drive.

They plan to dump her body in the wilderness.

I run a hand across my mouth and shove my phone into my pocket before whirling around to face her. She's off the car now, but she's still standing there, still waiting and watching me. She should've run from me by now, but she hasn't.

It's stupid of her, but I've been just as fucking stupid tonight in her presence. Maybe we're both completely fucking mad.

Still, I have to question it. "Why haven't you run?"

I stomp around to the side of the car and tug open the back door. I reach inside for my gym bag, thanking my past self for leaving it here instead of bringing it inside my apartment. I set it on the seat and unzip it as she comes around the side, standing behind me.

"I don't have anywhere to go. They're expecting me dead, aren't they?"

"Obviously." I find the pair of light gray sweatpants in my bag and pull them out, grateful I have something to change into after coming in my jeans like a fucking teenager.

"Then where would I go?"

I unbuckle my belt and tug at the button and zipper of my jeans.

"I'm not safe," she says. "Not anywhere. I might as well stay with you."

I shamelessly shove down my jeans and underwear, toeing off my tennis shoes as I do. She lets out a sweet little gasp as I expose myself right in front of her, and her short, ashen hair whips around her face as she spins to turn away.

I'm surprised by her sudden jolt of modesty after what

just happened, but I suppose she feels as overwhelmed by the crackle between us as I do. I quickly pull on my sweatpants, toss my soiled clothing into the gym bag, and shove it back down to the floorboard of the backseat.

"You can turn around. I'm dressed," I tell her as I kneel to retie my shoes.

I feel the gravity of her as she spins, and it tugs my chin upward with curiosity to gaze at her face. Even in the relative dark, I can see that her cheeks are flushed pink, and it makes my balls tighten.

I've already ruined one pair of pants tonight…

I rise and step closer, and she takes a hesitant step back. When I stop, though, she stops herself, too, pulling her shoulders back and stepping forward again, as though she needs to square off with me to maintain her dignity.

It's fucking cute.

"Was it him?" she asks. "On the phone… was it Benji Baker?"

"The Grave Digger himself. Yeah."

Her throat bobs as she swallows. "If you're not going to kill me, then maybe…" she hesitates, "Maybe you can protect me."

"Protect you?" I scoff. "What makes you think that the man hired to kill you would suddenly deflect just to protect you?"

"Because the man hired to kill me failed." Her head tilts condescendingly. "He failed and made me come in my jeans instead."

Well, fuck me.

The way she just lets the words tumble from her—affirming that she enjoyed what happened between us—makes me want her all over again. I've never fucking wanted someone this much.

"Please, Hendrix." Her grayish eyes soften and beg me beneath the glow of the lamp overhead. "I don't know what else to do, where else to go. I just… I need your help. Just get me through the night so I can testify tomorrow and then it will all be over."

My head snaps back. "Are you insane? You're not fucking testifying tomorrow."

"I have to. I can put him away. My lawyer said—"

"Your lawyer is a moron who's going to get you killed."

Her eyebrows lift as she chuckles, crossing her arms over her chest. "Killed by whom? They hired *you* to do it, and you failed."

Amused annoyance sets my jaw and I snap, "Angel, please." I reach out and wrap my fingers around the side of her neck, then tug her against me. Her warm, soft body crushes to mine, and her heat sinks through me. "I know you're not trying to goad me. Are you trying to get a rise out of me? Because you're on your fucking way."

Her lips twitch as she suppresses a smile. "I already got a rise out of you."

This girl can't be charming, too.

She's going to wreck me.

I slip my other arm around her waist and hold her close, unable to let go of her. "Don't be cute with me. This is serious. You don't understand the game you're playing with Benji."

Her hands snap to my chest, and she presses lightly. "I know it's not a game. That piece of shit ruined my life. He ruined my best friend's life, and then he ended her like she was *nothing*. Standing right in front of me, he just..." Her eyes shift to gaze off into the darkness beyond me. "He slit her throat like it was nothing... like she was nothing." Her eyes snap back to meet mine. "She wasn't nothing, Hendrix!"

I feel her muscles loosening their tension as it rises through her voice instead. She slumps into my hold, her hands slowly drifting across my chest and down my biceps— unconscious movement that makes my chest tighten and my cock twitch.

"She was like a sister to me, and he ruined her. He destroyed her life with that *fucking* drug, and I was just trying to save her. I just wanted to save her that night and I couldn't. I was too late." Her breath catches as tears cloud over the brown flecks in her gray eyes. "I was too late, and he killed her just because I came to take her home... just because I was *there*. It's... it's my fault. God, it's my fault. It's my fault she's dead!"

My hand slips up to cradle the back of her head and pull her down to my chest. My heart beats wildly as she lets go of her tears, soaking my hoodie. My grip tightens, the need to comfort and protect this sweet tiny thing floods my veins, and murderous rage for Benji Baker rushes right behind it.

I hold her for far longer than I should, longer than we have time to spare. But the longer I hold her, the stronger my resolve becomes.

I won't kill her… I *can't*.

But more than that, I already know she's ruined me. I already know I'll do whatever it takes to save her. I already know that she's going to be mine.

And no one takes what's mine.

CHAPTER SEVEN

Birdie

"**I HAVE TO** take you somewhere," Hendrix says when my tears have finally settled.

I slowly lift my head from his chest and pull back so I can look up at him. "Where? Why?"

"They want me to bring your body to a dump site."

"What?" Sickness rains down on me like a sudden downpour that startles me.

I jerk back and the abruptness of my movement catches him off-guard, forcing him to release me. I step back and look at him with widened eyes, though one of my hands still clutches his hoodie at the side of his waist.

Why do I cling to him?

What am I doing?

He's one of them.

"I have to take you there," he says.

I release him and take another step back. "No," I tell him, shaking my head and narrowing my eyes. "*No.* We have to flee. We have to run. We have to get the hell away from this place."

"I'm going to take you away from this place."

"To my *dump site?*" The words seem so informal, so crude, so horrifying to hear out loud.

My narrowed eyes gradually widen as my brain finally has a beat to catch up with everything that's happened tonight.

This is what he meant to do.

Hendrix was sent to kill me and take my body to a dump site. They were going to dispose of my remains. *He* was going to dispose of my remains, and here I am, losing myself to him like some lust-maddened fool. If he takes me to that dump site, Benji's men will do the job Hendrix failed to do.

"*No,*" I tell him firmly, holding my hands up as I take another step back.

"Birdie, I have to make an appearance. I have to show up. And I can't show up without you."

"*Fuck* no!"

"I have a plan."

"What plan? How could you possibly have a plan?"

"I just need you to get in the car with me, and I'll tell you on the way."

Oh, God.

Was this all an act?

Has this all been pretend?

Is he going to pawn the job off onto someone else at the

dump site because he just can't do it himself?

And I just let him use me to get off because of my physical attraction to him. I'm a fucking moron.

"Get the hell away from me!" I shout, moving backward.

He follows me. "Birdie, just get in the car."

"No!"

"Get in the car, Birdie."

"Stop saying my name!"

"Get in the *fucking* car!" His frustration rises to meet my fear.

This is it…

I can't let him take me to another location.

If I get in that car, it's over for me.

Finally—*finally*—I come to my senses, turn sharply, and run.

"Fuck!" I hear his footfalls on the pavement as he chases after me.

I have no sense of direction. No idea which way to go to find safety. We're in the middle of nowhere. There's nothing around, no one to help me. It doesn't really matter to me at this point if I can find safety, it only matters that I run—that I prove to myself that I'm not some weak-minded little girl who just gives into the warmth of a strong, beautiful man because he gave me a moment's attention. I have to run— though part of me wishes he'll catch me.

And it's not long before he does.

I yelp as he collides with my back, knocking me

forward with our shared momentum. His arms close around my waist, and I'm thankful that they do because my body lurches forward, bending as the pavement rises to meet me.

I throw my hands out to catch our fall, but he twists us, bringing us down onto our hips, though his body takes the brunt of the collision. Swiftly, he rolls, turning onto his back and bringing me over him with ease.

I clamp my hands around his wrists, digging my nails into his skin, fighting to shove his hands away as my heels kick at his shins.

"Fuck. Stop," he hisses.

He twists again, easily moving me with brute force—I can't match his height and strength, no matter how hard I fight. I've already learned this lesson several times tonight, yet here I am, still fighting.

This fight isn't the same, though.

This fight is final—it's my last chance to get away from this man, because I know I'll never get away from him again if he drives away. I don't think I'd have it in me to run again.

And worse, he's familiar now. I know him intimately, and there's something… unexpected between us.

I can already feel the fight in me fading the more I think, the more I let emotions and feelings get in the way. I have to remember who he is, what he was meant to do to me—what he *failed* to do to me.

Make him fail again.

I let go of his wrist as he spins us sideways, struggling

to get to his feet and pull me with him. He starts to stand with his arms still firmly around my waist, but I bend, letting my weight fall forward toward the pavement. As he bends over me, I jerk my elbow back into his gut. He groans and his grip loosens, though it doesn't loosen enough to let me fall away.

I do it again, bringing my elbow back hard and jabbing it into his hipbone.

"Ah, fuck," he groans again.

But his determination is stronger than mine.

He jerks me back and pulls me upright as he brings me to my feet. Though I manage to spin in his hold, pounding my fists against his chest, he holds me tight.

"Just stop it," he says. "I'm not going to hurt you."

"Fuck you," I spit. "I don't believe you. How could I fucking believe you?"

He bends at the knees, his arms—which are looped around my waist—shift to grip behind my knees. As he straightens, he lifts me right off my feet, tossing me over his shoulder with ease and fury.

I let out a pathetic squeak of protest—too surprised to scream, too impressed with his strength to fight. He stalks toward his car as I drop my palms to press against his lower back, my fingers fisting the fabric of his black hoodie to hold on as he carries me away like a sack of potatoes.

I should still be kicking, screaming, fighting, but I don't feel it anymore. I don't feel the urgency, the fear, the need to get away from him by any means necessary.

And honestly, that's the most frightening thing of all—feeling like I don't fear him anymore… like I can't fear him anymore… like being tossed over his shoulder like a rag doll makes me feel safer knowing that he's in control of me.

How can I fear him one moment and feel safe with him the next?

Who the hell is *he?*

Instead of looking out into the darkness behind us as he carries me, my eyes drop down, landing on his taut ass cheeks, hidden only by the fabric of his light gray sweatpants.

I'm mesmerized by the way his body moves as he walks. I'm suddenly overcome by the urge to let my hand slip lower down his back, to curl my fingers around those perfectly sculpted cheeks.

It's not fair that my body is attracted to his. It's not fair that he's gorgeous in his own imperfect way. It's not fair that his cold, demanding personality gives me emotional whiplash.

The sound of the door clicking open shakes me back to reality. He slips me back over his shoulder, sliding my body down the front of his, keeping me close to prevent me from getting away again—even though I'm not fighting him anymore. Our eyes meet as I land on my feet in front of him and raise my chin to look up at him.

With all the strength I can muster, I slap my hand across his cheek. I'm so goddamn angry at him for being one of them, for not doing his job and getting it over with quickly. I'm angry at him for his very existence because it's confusing the hell out of me.

His face turns away with the strike, then slowly, he looks back at me. He shifts closer, crowding against me, forcing my body into the gap made by the open door. "Get in," he demands with intense, wide eyes and lifted brows. "Get in the fucking car *right now*."

He presses forward and my body bends into the gap. I throw my arms out to try to brace myself against the frame.

"If you want to survive, you'll get in."

"I don't trust you."

"You don't have to. You just have to get in the car. If you don't, you're dead. They *will* send someone else."

I grit my teeth and tighten my grip, trying to pull myself out as his body forces me in. "No."

"Yes."

His hands snap out, wrap around my wrists, and pull them from the frame with a single, sharp tug. I lose my balance, falling into the gap, and he takes advantage to push me in faster.

My butt lands on the seat, and he bends, slipping one of his large palms beneath my legs to toss them in. I yelp as it spins me in the seat to face forward.

He reaches up to grab the seatbelt, tugging it across my chest and buckling it at my hip. My breath catches as his fingers graze my side. My hand moves on its own to snatch his wrist, and everything stops.

I stop.

He stops.

He just hovers there with his hand beside my hip, still gripping the buckle, though it's locked in place. His eyes turn to meet mine and the hard, dark edges suddenly soften.

My head thumps back against the headrest in defeat. He's won… he's won this battle with me, but the tightening in my chest tells me he could win all of them. The look in his gaze ends any fight I had left because I see so deeply. I see sincere desperation in the darkness of his eyes.

I see concern.

And then he kisses me. It shuts me up and stills me completely, stunning me with gentleness in the way he puts his lips on mine. The sweet softness feels like care and connection.

It *is* connection.

I'm connected to him now whether I want it or not.

But I do want it… I know I do.

Letting out a long, slow breath through my nose, I sink in the seat, letting him brush his tongue across my lips before parting for him. Our tongues lap, almost lazily, the heat of the fight twisting and turning into languid tasting. The kiss gradually fades with heated, heavy breaths, and his forehead touches mine.

"I don't know who you are, Birdie Collins," he whispers, pausing to lick his lips, gathering the lingering taste of mine.

"But I know I won't let them hurt you. I won't let them touch you. I just need you to let me save you."

I need to be saved.

He needs to save me.

And I know I'm going to let him.

CHAPTER EIGHT
Hendrix

"YOU'RE MINE NOW." The words slip out freely as a truth that makes no sense.

She *is* mine now, because I'm claiming her, but I don't know why I want her so much.

Her eyes lock on mine as she barely nods her silent agreement with our foreheads still touching. We're so close that even in the dim overhead light which shines with the car door still open, I can see the russet flecks in her gray eyes and how they brighten with her acknowledgment.

I couldn't tell you the color of my ex-girlfriends' eyes, my best friend, my sister, my dad… the most important people in my life at one moment or another, and I can't remember the color of their eyes.

But the gray and brown shades of Birdie's are already imprinted in my memory—plain, ordinary, but uniquely stunning all the same. Her eyes are expressive, glowing with brightness that somehow breaks through the neutral colors that would otherwise be considered drab.

I can't stop fucking staring.

I have to stop, though. I have to pull away, shut her door, walk around the car, and get in the driver's seat beside her. I turn over the engine and start driving, relief washing over me that she hasn't reached for her seatbelt and tried to jump out of the car yet.

I glance over at her as we pull through the empty lot and see her hands pressed against the seat on either side of her hips. She's staring forward, straight ahead, and she looks like she hasn't moved an inch since the kiss ended… like it froze her in time.

"You can relax, I'm not going to hurt you," I tell her, glancing between her and the dark road ahead.

"Okay," she replies softly.

Silence settles as I drive down unlit roads. Neither of us speak again until I pull onto the freeway. Traffic is sparse on the dark stretch of highway.

"I don't know anything about you," Birdie whispers.

She tensely shifts in her seat, her hands moving atop her thighs, fingers curling into the denim fabric of her jeans.

"What do you wanna know?"

Her head turns toward me, and though she's cloaked in shadow, I can still see the glow of her eyes—I can feel the spark of her soul shining through them, striking that fucking lightning bolt through my chest.

"Do you sell for them?" she asks.

I turn my head back to watch the black road. "No."

"Do you use?"

"What?"

"Numb. Do you use it?"

"No. I tried it once, but I don't use. I'm not a junkie."

"So, you don't sell. You don't use. Are you…? Do you know him?"

My eyes narrow in confusion, but then I realize who she means. "The Grave Digger? Yeah, you could say I know him. I owed him a favor."

"Is that what my life is? A favor that's owed?"

"It is to him. Your life means nothing to him."

I sense her eyes leave me and when I look over at her, I see her pull in a deep breath as she gazes out at the freeway. She trembles, her arms crossing, hands rubbing over her biceps. I reach over and crank up the heat a couple of degrees.

She speaks softly, though she doesn't look at me. "He killed my best friend right in front of me. He gave her that shit drug and it ruined her life. She was addicted to numb and obsessed with Benji. It was like he got his hands on her and she became a shell of a person. She used to be bright… fucking happy, you know? I don't know what she ever saw in him. I don't know how he dragged her down so fast. She thought he loved her, but he was just…" she pauses, "he was just using her."

My head is turning back and forth between the road and Birdie. I wish I could pull over so I could watch her as she speaks, but we're on borrowed time as it is.

"He uses everyone," I offer.

Her head snaps to look at me and catches me in a glance that holds my eyes. "Not the way he used Nikki… He broke her, ruined her, and then he took her life. He took her life to spite me. Because I tried to help her, wanted to make her see him for who he really is." She chuckles darkly, turning her head away. "Well, she finally saw the truth that night when he slit her throat. I had to watch the realization finally hit her as blood ran down her chest—" Her voice cracks on an impending sob.

"Hey, it's—"

"I have to put him away. I have to testify tomorrow."

I grip the steering wheel tighter. "That's not going to happen."

Her arms snap down and her body twists with fury to face me. "It has to! I have to put him away."

"No one is putting him away, least of all you. Fuck. Do you understand that it doesn't matter? Do you get that, Birdie? Your testimony wouldn't do shit."

"Then why did he send you to kill me?"

"Because he's a fucking narcissist," I snap, "and a goddamn sadist. He enjoys showing people how much power he has. Playing with lives is just entertainment for him. Your death is just a means of asserting his authority, but make no mistake, he doesn't need you dead to keep himself out of prison."

"That's bullshit. My lawyer promised me that if I testify,

he'll—"

"Lawyers can't promise shit, especially when it comes to the Senseless."

"I have to testify, Hendrix."

At the sound of my name, my palm moves, seeking to touch her cheek, drawn to her like a magnet. My hand finds her with ease, as if it's traveled the path to her a thousand times.

She gasps as my skin touches hers and a burst of static electricity ignites between my hand and her cheek. I brush my thumb across her chin, along the seam of her lips, coming to a stop at the dip of her upper lip.

"I don't think I can handle you saying my name like that, angel."

Everything stops and stills except for the car rushing forward into the night. I feel her breath over my thumb as she exhales with shallow pants through her nose.

I feel her eyes on me, but I keep mine on the road because I'm afraid that if I look at her, I'll have to kiss her again. I *want* to kiss her again. I want to do more than kiss her, but I have to keep driving.

She could lean back, turn in her seat, pull away from my touch, but she doesn't. She doesn't move, not as my thumb slips away, drawing the line across her lips to the opposite corner, not as my hand slips over her chin, sliding down to rest on her throat. I feel her swallow against my touch.

I don't know why she lets me hold her by the throat,

but the fact that she does makes me feel in control.

I *am* in control… except for the fact that I'm not.

I'm not in control of my reactions to her. She should be dead, and I should be home, but instead she's alive, and I'm risking my life to save her.

Nothing makes any sense tonight.

"I'm going to save you from him, but that means that we have to disappear. You won't be testifying tomorrow. You won't be going anywhere near that goddamn courthouse." My thumb absently strokes her skin as I speak, and she continues to remain still, continues to remain held by my touch—by choice, not by force. "We have to meet these men on time. I need to kill them, whether you like it or not. Benji will find out, but it will buy us a little time to get out of town."

"You can't just kill people."

"They're not people, Birdie. Remember that. They're Senseless, and they'd do the same to you in a heartbeat if it meant saving their own skin."

"You're Senseless, too." She leans forward instead of back, and I let my hand slip to the side of her neck, my thumb brushing the hollow of her throat. "You're one of them."

"I'm not. I know that doesn't make any sense, but I am *not* one of them. Like I told you, I owed them a favor."

"And you didn't finish the job."

I look over at her, and even in the dark, I can see the

connection her soul begs for behind her eyes. "I didn't finish the job."

I'm on fucking autopilot as my eyes fall to her lips to watch the way they part, calling to me, begging my tongue to slip inside and taste her.

My fingers curve around her neck to pull her closer as I lean forward to kiss her, quick and rough and sloppy. Her chin tilts upward as her tongue meets mine, lick for desperate lick. If I didn't know it before, I know it now—this strong, beautiful woman is going to wreck me.

And I'm going to let her… because what the fuck else do I have in my pathetic life?

She drags herself away, pulling back from me with a rush that lingers between us. "You should… you should watch the road." Her words are no more than a breath.

My lips curl to share a smile with her before I turn my attention back to the road, holding the steering wheel with one hand. The other slips over her shoulder and down her arm to snatch her small hand. I hold her hand tight over the gearshift, and I can feel her energy shifting and settling, surrendering to this gravity between us.

"You don't even know me." Her fingers curl, her small hand clinging to mine. "Why are you doing this for me?"

"I don't know how to answer that."

"Why should I trust you?"

"You don't really have a choice, do you? Either you trust me or you're on your own."

"I don't want to be on my own anymore…" Her words are nearly inaudible, but they punch me in the gut all the same.

"You won't be on your own if you stick with me."

"You can't just leave your life behind." Her grip is so tight that my hand aches.

"What life? The life where I'm indebted to the Senseless? Where Benji's gonna keep calling on me to do his bidding whenever he wants? Nah, I'm good leaving that shit behind. Besides, I'm fucked as soon as he finds out you're not dead. I'll have to flee, anyway." I pause. "Might as well take you along for the ride."

"I don't know if I can trust you."

"I don't know if I can trust you, either."

"I want to," she says. "I just don't know what else I can do."

She falls quiet and I let her silence surround us for a few oddly peaceful moments.

I lift one finger from her hand, pointing toward the glove box. "Open that, give me your cell phone."

"*My* cell phone?" She reaches forward with her free hand, pulling open the glove box, reaching in to snatch her phone. "How do you have this?"

"I took it before we left your house, and good thing I did. I need to make a phone call, and I can't do it on this fucking burner phone Merrick gave me."

"Merrick?"

"My boss." I glance over at her and see confusion dip her brow. "Think of Benji as the CEO. Merrick is…" I pause, thinking of the best analogy. "He'd be like the regional director of distribution. He oversees pockets of distributors. He's one of several—Benji's eyes and ears on the ground."

"So, he's probably tracking that phone."

"It's off now, so I don't think he can. But they'll definitely trace my calls. That's why we need to use yours."

"Who are you gonna call?"

"Someone who can help us disappear."

I recite the phone number to her from memory—the only place this number will ever be stored. It's a safe line that my buddy Nico set up, only to be used for emergencies. And this is a fucking emergency if I've ever had one.

She puts the phone on speaker, letting go of my hand to hold it up for me. I can see her watch me carefully, concern over whether she can trust me still etched in the dip of her eyebrows.

The phone rings three times, and then someone picks up without saying a word, just as I expected. Nico wouldn't speak and give himself away until he knows who's calling him.

"It's Hendrix," I say.

I hear the huff of his breath as he exhales with relief. "Shit, man, where the fuck are you?"

"I didn't kill her."

"I know you didn't kill her. We *all* know. *Benji* fucking

knows."

"What?" I feel my forehead wrinkle with confusion. "No. He doesn't know. I just talked to him. I told him she's dead. He told me to take her to a dump site in Allegheny—"

"It's a setup, dumbass. He's going to kill you both when you get there."

"How the fuck does he know?"

"Because you're on the fucking nightly news, X. Benji had one of his guys sell the story, even gave them your picture. They're calling you a cop killer, saying you kidnapped the brave woman who was going to testify against the Senseless."

"Fuck!" I bang my fist against the steering wheel.

"Everyone in the tri-state area will know when they wake up in the morning and watch the news. X… you're fucked."

"Oh, my God," Birdie mutters.

"Fuck. Is that her?" Nico asks. "Is she really alive and with you? What the hell is going on?"

"Nico, listen. You have to help us, both of us. Can you help us disappear?"

He sighs. "Shit. Yeah. Of course, I can."

"What do we do? Where do we go?"

"Are you sure you want to do this? If I help you both, then that's it. Your life here is done. You have to cut ties with everyone you know. Are you prepared to do that? Is *she*?"

I look over at her and catch her wide eyes. She stares at me with parted lips, which seem hesitant to respond.

I hold her gaze. "I told you that the only way out of this for you is death, and I meant it. They'll kill you… or we can beat them to it and end our lives ourselves. We'll have to become new people, live new lives."

"How do I make a decision like that? I'm scared," she admits.

"So am I."

"There's no other choice?"

I shake my head. "No. And I'm sorry about that, I really am. I'm sorry I put you in this position. But if he hadn't sent me to kill you—"

"He would've sent someone else, and I'd already be dead."

"Yeah."

"I can't testify. I can't go back to my life." She chews on the corner of her lip nervously, and I feel like I can sense her heartache, like I can feel her tears burning behind her eyes, and it makes my chest ache.

I can't imagine what this feels like for her, to have her entire world literally crashing down around her. It's dangerous that I already care about her so fucking much.

Her eyes flick up to meet mine. "What do I do?" she asks, and the ache in my chest releases, fading into heat that warms my heart.

She waits, watching me, expecting me to respond. She wants me to tell her what to do, and though she probably wouldn't admit it—though it makes no fucking sense—I know it means that in some way, she trusts me.

"We choose to run," I tell her. "Together. We focus on saving ourselves, get the fuck out of here, and figure out the rest later."

Her head bobs, turning away to look out at the road. I wait for her to come to the same conclusion because I already know she will.

What other choice do we have?

She turns back to look at me, and I try to keep my eyes on her as much as I can while still speeding down the road. "I suppose this wouldn't be the first time I'm putting my life in your hands," she says.

I'm grateful for her concession, grateful that I don't have to tie her up and put her inside the trunk again to get her out of this place safely—I'd do it if I had to, but I prefer her consent.

I sigh with relief that I can focus on keeping us both alive. "Tell us where to go, Nico."

CHAPTER NINE

Birdie

HENDRIX PARKED HIS car near a wooded area in this small town I've heard of but never visited, probably an hour outside of Pittsburgh. His friend Nico told us to park a mile away from the motel he booked for us and walk there, keeping the car out of sight so it's harder for them to find us if they're looking.

I don't know if we can trust his friend, but I don't know what else to do at this point. I have to have some faith or else hope is lost entirely. It's what I have to focus on while I'm so overwhelmed by the torrent of emotions storming through me.

I'm furious that I can't testify.

I'm sorrowful that I can't give Nikki justice.

I'm numb about leaving my life behind.

I'm energized and wild-eyed at Hendrix's side.

Hendrix reaches out as we walk, snatching my hand in his grip. His fingers shift and lace through mine before he squeezes, holding onto me as though he's afraid I'll pull away.

But I can't pull away... I'm already locked in, tangled into his life, which is twisted through mine, fastened to a future I didn't know would exist before tonight.

My heart kicks up a steady rhythm as I squeeze back, longing for whatever this strange connection is between us—between me and my would-be killer. We're both about to leave our lives behind, and I can't think of a more frightening way to form a forever bond with someone... aside from the bond between murdered and murderer.

We pass through a dark parking lot on our way to the motel, trying to stay away from the main road. There's hardly any traffic this late, and it's dark aside from the single traffic light along the road parallel to us, which we've already passed. The yellow light flashes with an eerie, rhythmic glow as we walk together, the decrepit two-story motel just half a parking lot ahead of us.

"It's funny..." I whisper. "Normally I'd avoid walking through empty parking lots at night with strange men that I hardly know."

He lets out a short chuckle. "Do you often have the opportunity to walk through empty parking lots at night with strange men?"

"This is a first for me."

"First for me, too," he says.

"A night of firsts I'm certain I won't forget."

He glances over at me as he pulls me along to keep up

with his long strides. "Night's not over yet."

"Right," I swallow, my throat suddenly dry.

Something about his tone makes me wonder what he really means. If we follow Nico's instructions, we're going to sit quietly in a motel room until he comes to us after sunrise...

So what other firsts could there possibly be?

His thumb brushes the backs of my knuckles, sending a spark of electricity across my skin.

My eyes are fixed on him as we close the distance from this empty lot to the nearly empty one in front of the motel. I see his eyes flicker to dart a furtive glance in my direction, his chest rising heavily as he takes in a deep breath before falling again.

I hold an unexpected flurry of hope between our pressed palms, a tiny ball of electrical heat that begs for more touching behind a closed door.

Oh, God. I'll be alone with him behind a closed door.

The red fluorescent letters on the sign in the parking lot spell out "MOTEL," though the "O" blinks and flickers incessantly. Hendrix stops us for a moment on the patch of grass dividing one parking lot from the other. He turns his head to look around us, taking in our surroundings—and I suppose looking for any obvious threats.

I look around, too, and though I'm sure I don't know as much about the Senseless as Hendrix does, I know that I don't have a stab of instinct or anxiety telling me that something's wrong.

"Come on," he finally says, then takes off on a jog, pulling me along behind him.

We run across the small lot, passing behind a lone, empty vehicle parked in front of one of the motel rooms on the first level. I see the lights are on in the room right in front of it.

We reach the lobby door, and he releases my hand to open it—his gym bag held in the other hand. As I step through, he quickly snakes his arm around my waist instead. His warmth seeps into me as he tucks me in against his side, fingers wrapping around the side of my waist and digging in protectively… possessively.

He quickly checks us in using some fake name and pays in cash. I didn't even know you could get a hotel room without a credit card anymore, but based on the looks of this place, there might be a charge-by-the-hour rate, so maybe the anonymity of cash is warranted.

We get a key and Hendrix wastes no time shuffling me through the door. We turn and walk along the sidewalk that lines the doors to the first-floor rooms, turning a sharp right and walking toward the lone car in the lot.

Hendrix subtly slows our pace as we approach that room, his guard understandably on high alert. The curtains are drawn, so no one in the room can see us, but then we also can't see who's inside the room.

For a moment, I think he's going to stop, but his

fingertips dig deeper into my flesh. "Come on," he whispers just before quickening our pace.

We move past the curtain-drawn window, rushing by, but then the door suddenly clicks open just as we're about to cross it.

I startle and scream, a quick sharp yelp scraping from my throat. Hendrix startles, too, but he doesn't scream uselessly. He drops his bag and shoves me behind him, bending as if he's going to pounce and attack. We both jump when someone walks out through the door...

My hands are on Hendrix's back, fisting the fabric of his hoodie as I peek around him. A woman with tangled hair steps out, wearing a crop top, mini-skirt, and ridiculously high heels. She's folding a wad of cash and stuffing it into her clutch.

We both blow out a breath of relief.

"Fuck," Hendrix mutters.

The woman stops in front of us, looks us up and down appraisingly, and says, "I'd give you cuties a two-for-one discount. Cash only. You interested?"

I slap my hand over my mouth to cover my shock and the nervous laugh that threatens to burst from my lungs.

"No, thanks." Hendrix bends to grab the bag, then turns to reach for me, once again wrapping his arm around my waist and pulling me close.

My skin tingles from the jolt of adrenaline when she opened that damn door, rippling energy through my body that's desperate to explode as anxious laughter.

We walk past her, Hendrix keeping himself between us—keeping me safe. I glance around them both to peek into the room as we pass, and I see a man lying back on the bed, his pants down around his ankles and an empty can of beer resting in his hand. He's asleep—the sound of snoring carries out through the door—and the laugh I was trying to hold back erupts.

Hendrix's hand leaves my waist, his arm slipping around my neck and his palm covering my mouth.

"Shh," he whispers as we walk past. "Don't draw attention." His voice sounds so serious, but a quick glance at his face shows me the twist of his lips as he tries to suppress a smile.

That smile—his humor at a time like this—shows me a different part of him, and I genuinely want to see every part of him.

We keep walking until we're almost at the far corner of the building, stopping in front of the second to last door.

Hendrix releases me long enough to unlock it with the key. Then he reaches behind me to place his hand on the small of my back, pushing me past the threshold. Once inside, he slams the door shut behind us. He locks the knob, turns the deadbolt, and secures the chain lock.

I sigh, noting the single king-sized bed in the middle of the room. There's a set of drawers in front of it and a television set atop that. There's a bathroom straight ahead, and Hendrix goes straight for it.

He drops his gym bag on a chair, then pushes the bathroom door open cautiously before entering and looking around. I stand in place, rubbing my palms over my arms. With the silence and relative safety of being behind a locked door, the gravity of our situation is starting to hit me again.

The laughter is gone, replaced by an overwhelming prickle of unfamiliarity. I'm in a room I've never been in, at a motel I've never been to, in a town I've never visited, with a man I've only known for a night.

Nervous energy crawls up inside me, settling uncomfortably. I press a palm to my chest, willing my pounding heart to calm the fuck down.

Hendrix sighs, coming back out from the bathroom. "No window, that's good. Single point of entry. I think we'll be safe here for a while."

"If they really wanted to get through that door, they could."

Our heads turn at the same time, and our eyes meet suddenly, intensely.

There's a silent beat—a pause, not a hesitation—that acts like a reset. It's like his dark eyes burrow inside me and push a button in my soul that powers off the fear and anguish of the hours before. It reboots my system, turns me back on, reprograms the nervous energy into something oddly... pleasant.

"Yeah," he murmurs a moment before he moves, "but

they'd have to get through me first."

I gasp, taking a step back as he marches toward me, closing the distance between us in three long strides. My eyes don't leave his as his hands come up, as his palms grip my cheeks, as he tilts my head back and bends to kiss me.

Oh...

Our lips part and our tongues meet eagerly, both of us moaning with the relief of time and space and the relative appearance of safety.

God, I want him.

I want him so much it aches, and I don't care that I don't understand why. It only matters that I want him, that he wants me, and that we both urgently need a distraction from reality.

He pushes into me, walking me backward until I hit the wall beside the door. My palms slap back against the wall on either side of my hips as he presses me to it, his body a hard line that refuses to bend.

His tongue sweeps mine with a thick, flat lick as he turns his head to deepen the kiss. Immediately, my mind drifts to imagine him licking me that way between my legs.

My core clenches, tugging pleasure straight through me, and the kiss breaks as I puff out a heavy breath. But his lips don't leave me. He kisses a line along my jaw, to the spot behind my ear, his hips pressing forward as his teeth surprise me with a small nip.

"I want you so fucking much." His voice trembles and

he plants a palm on the wall above my head, those hips pinning me in place as they grind against me. "I need to know what it feels like to be inside you, angel."

My eyes flutter as I try to open them against the overwhelming lust this stranger makes me feel.

We won't be strangers for long.

Soon, all we'll have is each other.

I'm leaving my life behind, and so is he. Though it scares me, the fear just seems to heighten the need. We'll have to depend on each other and we'll need to know each other. I want to know him… I *need* to know him deeply.

I breathe heavily, turning my head to grant him better access to my neck as his lips sweep down. "Touch me. Make me come. I just…" I pause as a shudder of need bounces up my spine, "I just need to forget for a while."

His hand slips beneath the hem of my shirt. "I won't let you forget this."

I flinch as his fingers touch my skin, skimming up my belly, quickly seeking my breast. We both groan and my shoulders drop in relief as his warm, large palm curves around the mound, digging into my flesh as he squeezes.

My hand slips between our bodies, wrapping around his cock through his sweatpants. He groans and trembles, a pulse of need thrumming through his body.

"Fuck…*fuck*," he mutters into the crook of my neck as I stroke him through the fabric.

I could feel how hard he was when we dry fucked

against his car, but I didn't realize how big he was. Through the sweatpants, I feel *everything*. I can feel his length, his girth…

My pussy clenches at the thought of taking him inside me. Wetness pools as I imagine how full I'll feel when he fucks me.

"Hendrix…" I moan, my head thumping back against the wall, my hips grinding forward against the back of my hand as I play with him. "Let me have it…"

Reckless passion draws our lips together as we both seek relief through our rolling hips. Our eager mouths meet roughly but slip and slide as smoothly as our licking tongues.

His hands find my hips, quickly tracing the hem of my jeans to the button. His nimble fingers pop it open, and I gasp with need as he tugs down the zipper. His forehead drops to meet mine as the kiss breaks, but somehow it becomes something far more intimate.

My eyes slowly flutter open to meet his heated stare. "You're so fucking beautiful, angel."

A smile touches my lips as I put my hands over his, encouraging him to push my jeans and underwear down. "I like it when you call me that."

"Then I'll call you that when you make me come." His hands slip down my body, pulling my clothes with them as he lowers to his knees in front of me.

He tugs off my shoes and I step out of my jeans and panties, standing bare before him. It feels odd to only be half-naked, so I quickly tug my shirt over my head, tossing it to the side. His eyes dart from my face to my chest as I reach behind me to unhook my bra, letting the straps fall from my shoulders before throwing it aside.

My soul shivers as his gaze scans my flesh. He rubs a hand over his mouth as his eyes brighten with hunger, coming to life as if he's been waiting forever to see me bare.

I tug my bottom lip between my teeth as his hands move up my sides, his eyes casting a heated trail across my skin as he drinks me in. His hands roam all over me, the warmth of his stroking fingers leaving a cold trail of goosebumps behind them.

All at once, his hands snake around me, palms curving around my ass cheeks. He grips me hard and tugs my hips from the wall, but before I can so much as gasp, his mouth meets the curls that trail to my sex. My hands snap down to land on his head, tangling in his raven hair.

"You're perfect," he mutters against my curls.

He drags his tongue all the way up to my belly button, and I sigh from the tease of pleasure. I grip his hair, holding his face against me as he kisses his way back down.

"Hendrix…"

After moments of pure bliss, he pulls back and looks up at me, his hair tousled from my grip and eyes burning with desire. "I want to taste you."

The way he pants as he watches me—waiting for my response like a beggar on his knees— makes wetness slick my core, and my pussy clenches as my knees go weak.

His eyes widen as my knees bend involuntarily, taking it as a signal of how much I want his tongue to taste me—and that's exactly what it is. His hands stretch, thumbs reaching around to dig into my pelvic bone as he grabs hold of me, pulling me down to the floor.

He lays back as he drags me down, and I drop to my knees, straddling his waist.

His tongue runs over his lips. "Sit on my face."

"What?"

His legs bend beneath me. I feel his thigh raising with his knee, nudging against my back as his hands dig into my waist and jerk me forward.

"Climb up here, straddle my head, and sit on my fucking face, Birdie."

"You want me to—"

"Fuck my face."

My eyes widen as his eyes narrow, his gaze focused with intention. He tugs, urging me to climb over him, and I let him guide me. I shuffle forward on my knees, a punch of worry stealing my attention as I realize how much of myself I'm giving to him.

I'm bare.

I'm completely exposed and vulnerable.

I'm literally open wide for him to take what he wants, to admire, to explore, to judge… maybe to reject.

I reach out to place my palm on the wall beside me,

immobile as I hover above him. I close my eyes to center myself, but I feel the frenetic energy flow from Hendrix beneath me in waves.

His arms wrap around my thighs, and I feel a finger caress smoothly down my slit. "Fuck," he mutters.

"Oh, God." My face contracts as I lean on my hand against the wall.

"You're dripping." He circles my opening and gathers wetness, then drags his finger to my clit. "Birdie," he rasps, "let me taste you. *Please*, fucking let me."

I whimper at the desperation in his tone, which draws out my own. With courage I didn't know I had, I adjust my position, slowly spreading my knees and lowering my bare pussy toward his face.

It takes more bravery than I would have imagined to do this, considering how much bravery I've already had to show tonight. I'm truthfully shocked at my complete lack of inhibition from being in a position like this with someone I barely know. Hovering just above him, I wait for his tongue.

"*Sit*, angel. Cover my face. Take my fucking breath away."

"I can't—"

"I need you to." His hands quickly rise to my hips, and he tugs me down until I'm literally *sitting* on his face.

I try to lift away—legitimately concerned I'll suffocate him—but his fingers dig deeper, holding me down as he groans with his lips mashed against my pussy.

"Holy fucking… Oh, *God*…"

His tongue licks flat across my slit from back to front, dipping inside and swirling around my inner walls.

I tremble.

I hear him inhale deeply, then groan again as he takes in my scent. His fingers are nearly painful where they hold me, clutching my flesh, pulling me forward.

He wants me to fuck his tongue.

My head rolls, dropping toward my shoulder as my back arches. I let my weight fall just as he begged me for it. His tongue assaults me brutally—beautifully—twisting and rolling and licking every inch of me that he can reach.

As I grind down against his face, I feel the tip of his nose bump against my clit, and *fuck*, it feels good. I want to grind against it, make myself come, but I'm still hesitant because I'm afraid I might actually break his nose—I know myself, and I tend to be a little overzealous when I'm on top.

But Hendrix doesn't know that about me yet. I feel like I want him to know me that way. I want him to know how I'll respond to every touch, every whisper. I want him to know what makes me come, and how to know when I need it rough and when I need it gentle.

Lost in my thoughts, I suddenly realize how fast I'm rocking, how heavily I'm sitting. I lift away, shifting back so I can look down at him and make sure he's still breathing. His eyes are hooded, my wetness spread across his cheeks. His lips part when I pull away from him, and he's panting, fighting for air.

He licks his swollen lips. "More."

My stomach clenches desperately.

I start to move backward, aching to fuck him, prepared to free his cock and impale myself on it. But he stops me with a groan, quickly flipping me onto my back and looking up at me from beneath his lashes.

"I wasn't finished," he growls.

His mouth comes down on me, but his eyes don't leave mine. I push up onto my elbows to watch him as he licks and laps with intention.

His stare, the way he watches me as he eats me out, is *everything*. He watches me with hunger, with gratitude, and it makes me feel powerful. I met him when he was determined to end my life, but now I feel like he's *giving* me life in the way he wants to please me.

I want to keep watching him, but the way my clit swells under the flick of his tongue makes the world fade away. My head drops back, hair dangling toward the carpet, and my eyes drift shut. My thighs clench around his ears as he drives me toward release, alternating between sucking and licking.

More than anything else, it's the way his arms are wrapped around my thighs that overwhelms me—I'm sure I'll have bruises where the tips of his fingers prod into my flesh. It's the way he holds me like he just can't let go, like he *refuses* to let go until I give him what he wants… and what he wants is for me to come on his face.

I gasp, lifting my head and looking down at him as I feel the tightening in my core. His tongue swirls and presses, his lips clamp down and suck in a blinding rhythm. My thighs twitch, clenching against his cheeks, and his biting fingers dig deeper.

"Hendrix," I beg.

He groans and the vibration against my clit sets me off, sparking with a sharp tingle that quickly erupts in perfect, relieving pleasure.

"Oh, my God," I mutter, tension breaking and causing my legs to release their death hold on his head.

The heels of my hands touch my forehead as my fingers comb into my hair, and I fight to catch my breath. Hendrix sits up on his knees to peel off his hoodie and the shirt beneath it, tossing them to the floor, though I don't know where they land.

All I see are washboard abs—completely unreal—and the gorgeous face of the first man who ever made me come from oral.

He hooks his fingers in the waistband of his sweatpants, tugging them down. His hard cock springs free, standing long and proud and impossibly thick.

Slipping his sweatpants down his knees, he climbs over me, my heart beating faster as he comes closer. His palms touch the ground on either side of my head as he stares down at me, rolling his hips forward so I can feel his erection against my swollen pussy.

He bends over me, kissing the corner of my mouth, my cheek, my jaw, down the side of my neck. His hair is soft against my cheek, and I can't help but wrap my arms around him to tangle my fingers in the dark strands.

He kisses a spot on my neck that feels tender to the touch, and I wince, surprised at the slight ache.

"I'm sorry," he whispers, kissing the spot again.

"Huh?" I'm a little lost in the blurred line between pleasure and pain.

He pulls back and cradles the side of my neck in his palm, brushing his thumb across that tender spot again. "I bruised you."

He bruised me… When?

Right… When he tried to strangle me.

I swallow hard as I lift my eyes to meet his. I think I should expect to see darkness staring back at me, but I only see regret as his hand slips up my neck, thumb drawing a line along my jaw.

His eyes drop to my lips. "I'm so glad I fucked up that job," he says, then kisses me deeper than I've ever been kissed before.

I gasp into his mouth, his cock punching inside me at the same moment as his tongue. His intrusion is quick and deep, my inner walls stretching to accommodate his thickness.

I'm filled with him—as much as I can be—and it feels

so good. His face is slick as he consumes me with his sloppy kiss, wetness from between my legs smearing from his face to mine.

His teeth grab my bottom lip and tug, then release. His head bows over mine, our foreheads touching, and it feels far more intimate than his cock buried to the hilt inside me.

I don't know what it is about the feeling of his forehead against mine, but it makes me feel so connected with him, like our brain waves share an unexpected kind of synergy that sparks between us.

"I should have asked first, but I couldn't wait. I don't have a condom."

"I don't care," I tell him honestly. "I should care, but I don't. I could be dead right now if it wasn't you who showed up at my house tonight. I could be dead, but I've never felt more alive, and I really don't give a fuck about a condom right now."

He shifts his hips, going deeper, and I think I can feel him pulsing against my soul, trying to punch right through and cause irreparable damage—the kind that can only be mended by merging with another.

An audible breath escapes me as my back arches, my chin tilts, my lips brush his.

"You feel so good," he whispers. "So fucking perfect. I can't pull out."

I hold his cheeks between my palms. "Then don't. Please don't. Come inside me, please."

I silently beg for another kiss, sweeping my lips lightly over his, breathing against him and catching his breath against me. He obliges softly, gently kissing me, slowly slipping his tongue inside for a languid, swirling taste.

We moan and grind together with him inside me. I wonder if I've ever felt this good before—this intense, this heated, this passionate.

I know I haven't.

Our kiss breaks as our need grows, as grinding turns into slow thrusting, which threatens to devolve to wild fucking.

I want that.

I want the heat, the lust… hell, I want the violence of it. It would be fitting considering all the violence that's existed between us from the moment we met.

"Fuck me," I demand, lifting my hips to encourage movement.

He looks down at me with the most striking combination of darkness and passion—it makes me feel reckless for being with him this way. But he makes me forget about what-ifs and consequences, and the danger of everything that swirls around us makes me high.

Panting, he fucks me—hard, but slow—thrusting with complete, deep strokes. He rears back, sitting up sharply on his knees, running his hands up my thighs. He grabs my hips and tugs me, the cheap carpet scraping across my back as he angles me, my ass resting against strong thighs.

I hook my ankles together behind his back as he slips inside me again, his cock slamming into my G-spot perfectly. I groan as he hits it hard, determination sharpening his features.

"I need you to come again, angel."

I'm not the girl who can come twice, and I don't come from penetration alone. But it's not just between my legs that he fills me… and maybe that's the difference.

I can feel something building—a wild pulsing, an insistent throbbing as he fucks me in the simplest, dirtiest way. He licks his thumb, bringing it down and finding my clit far too easily. He rubs back and forth in a steady rhythm—as if he already knows exactly what I like—and I feel it *everywhere*.

My pussy clenches around his cock, and I see the way he feels it as his jaw tenses and he grits his teeth.

"Come for me," he commands.

I'm lost to the pressure building between us, my head rolling from side to side, teeth digging into my bottom lip. My body squirms to get away from this overwhelming tingle that ripples through my clit.

As my body shifts, he moves with me, unrelenting with his rhythm and force. The crude sound of skin slapping skin surrounds us, mingling with our breaths and moans to create a perfectly sinful chorus.

"Fuck," he shudders, "I'm gonna come… I need you to come with me."

"I... *Yes.*" My hips lift, muscles tightening as I feel it start, the devastating pressure that pulses, then snaps. "*Yes!*" I cry out as he pummels me.

"Fuck, angel, yes." His cock swells inside me, throbbing, and my orgasm matches the rhythm of its pulse. "Ah, that's good... you're so fucking good," he grits. "*Fuck yes...*" Three more urgent thrusts and I feel the warmth of his liquid spill inside me.

My legs shake through the last dregs of the longest orgasm I've ever had. He pushes my knees apart, making my feet drop with a *thump* to the floor. Then he bends, kissing me deeply.

His fingers find their way into my hair, the heel of his hand pressed to my cheek as he shifts and props his weight up on one elbow.

His body covers mine completely.

Every sense is stimulated.

I chuckle against his lips as it pops into my head just how completely *senseless* we are together. This connection between us, the fact that I just let the man who tried to kill me fuck me without any protection... the notion that we have to run away together to have any chance at a life beyond tonight.

We're senseless... How ironic.

He pulls back, lets a soft smile touch his lips as his eyes flicker across my face. "You're mine, Birdie Collins."

Our smiles fade together as our eyes shift through each

other into thoughtful gazes.

I nod as his thumb softly brushes along my bottom lip, and I tell him with acceptance, "I know."

"I NEED YOUR words. I need your thoughts, your mind… I need to know this pull between us isn't just physical."

His eyes hood, staring deep into mine and making my heart flutter. "What was it before? Against my car?"

We're still on the floor, laying on our sides, limbs tangled. His fingers play through mine as we watch each other, both of us curious how we made the leap from fighting for our lives to fucking like there's no tomorrow.

"Something more…" The words slip quietly from my lips, and I don't even understand what they mean.

But it *was* something more—more than flesh, more than sheer desperation. I'd felt some kind of connection with him beyond the physical in those moments. The same kind of connection I'm feeling now in the way we watch each other… in the way he bares his soul to me through his eyes.

"Do you think it was meant to be me tonight?" The gravity in his question hangs heavily between us.

"I don't believe in meant to be," I tell him, honest thoughts from what I assumed were my core beliefs.

But shit, as soon as I say the words, they sound wrong. They sound stupid. They sound like everything I thought

I knew was wrong. Yet I feel like I have to explain myself, defend what I'm saying.

"I can't believe in things like fate and destiny," I tell him. "If I did, I'd have to believe that Nikki was always meant to die the way she did. And I can't believe that... I won't. People make choices, and sometimes those choices put them in bad places."

He watches my face carefully as I speak, no anger or judgment present in his expression. "Why can't both things exist together, Birdie?"

My brow furrows as I look from his eyes to his lips and back again. "I don't understand how they could."

"What if some things are meant to be, but our choices can change the course of destiny when our fates are revealed to us?"

My eyes widen a little as I take a deep breath, my tongue running across my suddenly dry lips. "I don't—"

"What if fate decided you and I were always meant to meet tonight?" He shifts, moving impossibly closer, every inch of him touching every inch of me. "What if fate decided I should kill you? What if *you* changed the course of our destiny with the way you fought me, with the way you showed me what your soul was made of? It was your passion, Birdie. You made me change my mind. What if we were both meant to die tonight, but that fate changed because we decided we could leave everything we knew behind and start new lives? And what if we could only start new lives by doing it together?"

I sigh, my body melting with the way my connection to him deepens with each precious word. There *is* something more, something deeper between us that insists on being acknowledged. I place my hand on his cheek and let my fingers slip back to comb into his thick, black hair.

"Didn't you feel it?" he asks. "Didn't you feel just how much our souls were fated to meet with my cock buried deep inside you?"

I let out a whimper, my lips snapping to meet his as if they were tugged there by force.

I *did* feel it… I *do*.

And I don't understand it at all.

"This is insane," I whisper against his mouth.

"Does this feel like insanity to you?"

"It doesn't feel that way to you?"

"Most of my life has been one insane event after the other, but not this, angel. This doesn't feel like insanity."

"Then what does it feel like?"

He sighs, stroking his hand down the side of my head. "It feels like clarity. It feels like destiny."

He rolls me onto my back and bends over me so his lips sweep the shell of my ear as he mutters, "I think a demented god decided to clip your wings and throw you from heaven, but I'm going to show you how you were always meant to fall, angel… That you were always meant to sin with me."

"To save you?"

He kisses across my cheek. "Yes, angel. We're meant to save each other."

CHAPTER TEN
Hendrix

I WATCH BIRDIE from the bathroom while I brush my teeth with a toothbrush I got from the manager in the lobby. She's fully dressed again, despite my protest. She sits perched on the foot of the bed, sitting as if she's prepared to jump up and flee—just like a bird perched on a branch ready to fly away.

I guess her parents chose her name well. There is something rather bird-like about her delicate features and small stature, but she's no canary.

She's a motherfucking hawk.

Watching her, I smile to myself. Her eyes are glued to the television, waiting for the next news cycle to start so she can see what's being said about us, and about Benji and the trial.

She chews the side of her thumb and her knee bounces as she watches. I don't like when she's nervous because it makes me nervous, too. I bend and spit, rinse the brush, and put it down so I can rush to sit next to her.

She turns her head to look at me as I lower beside her, eyes starting low and raking their way up my bare chest. When she meets my eyes, she gives me a sweet little smile before tugging her bottom lip between her teeth. I reach up to tuck her tangled hair behind her ear, messy from fucking.

"You don't need to be nervous with me," I tell her. "I'm not going to let anyone hurt you."

Her gaze shifts, and I rest my palm against her cheek, thumb brushing over her skin—I feel completely powerless against the need to touch her.

She opens her mouth like she's going to speak, but then snaps her head away to look at the television when the familiar jingle of a local news station plays, capturing her attention.

I want it back.

I want her attention on me, but I know we should listen. It's smart that she wanted to tune in. We'll have an easier time hiding from the world if we know what we're really up against.

A blonde female newscaster speaks in a professional tone. "Breaking news coming in on the case against The Grave Digger, a man who has managed to remain above prosecution from his actions as the leader of a local drug ring. The Grave Digger, otherwise known as Benjamin Baker, is said to be responsible for the loss of thousands of lives in the four short years since he allegedly crafted a new synthetic drug called numb. Local police departments in the tri-state area have been after him for years but were unsuccessful in putting together a case against him. While many leaders of the Senseless cartel have been prosecuted for crimes, Benjamin Baker has remained elusive.

"In a surprise twist, a shocking homicide nearly ended the Grave Digger's reign. Six months ago, twenty-three-year-old graduate student Nikki Chambers was brutally murdered…"

Birdie reaches over without peeling her eyes away from the television, grabbing hold of my hand. I pull her palm onto my lap.

"…until a friend of Ms. Chambers came forward, informing police that she had witnessed the murder. Twenty-two-year-old Birdie Collins…"

Birdie squeezes my hand as her picture comes up on the screen.

Fuck.

She looks bright and happy in the photo they show. I glance over at her, regarding the worry etched on her features, the anxiety and unsurety that shadows each beautiful line on her face. I'd like to see her smile like she does in the photo on the screen… I'd like to be the one to spark it.

This girl could change me.

She could ruin me.

She could make me want to be a better man.

I already know she's getting whatever the fuck she wants from me.

I realize how much I've missed on the news when she snaps at me to get my attention, "Hendrix!"

I turn my head sharply to watch.

"...but according to our sources, charges against the Grave Digger have been dropped by the prosecution as of 10:52 this evening for the murder of Nikki Chambers—"

"*What?*"

Birdie leaps to her feet, shaking her hand from my grip and stepping toward the television as if she could reach out and wrap her hand around the newscaster's throat.

"Our sources state that the prosecution has decided it cannot move forward with pursuing these charges. When pressed to cite a reason for dropping these charges so unexpectedly, they declined to comment."

She turns on screen toward a male newscaster sitting beside her, and he takes over. "That's right, Kelly, and our investigative news team has been hot on the case since these reports came in. We highly suspect that the dropped charges may have some correlation with the kidnapping of the key witness in their case. Birdie Collins was taken from her home earlier this evening. Her police detail was found dead in the basement of her home, and Ms. Collins has been unaccounted for since. An anonymous source reported twenty-four-year-old Hendrix Hadid as a potential suspect."

My fucking mug shot pops up on screen... from that one stupid fucking time I tried numb and got arrested for a petty crime. And that's the goddamn image they're blasting all over the media.

Birdie glances at me over her shoulder, but I can't look at her. I'm fucking terrified to witness her judgment—I'm nervous she'll see me as a criminal rather than a man. I don't want to see fear in her eyes. I drop my face into my hands with elbows on my knees.

"Police suspect that Mr. Hadid is armed and dangerous. If you see him, do not approach. He is wanted for questioning about the whereabouts of Birdie Collins and the murder of Officer David Hamilton." They show mine and Birdie's pictures side-by-side on the screen. "Please call 9-1-1 if you spot either of these persons of interest as police suspect they are still in the area."

As they move on to the next news story, I feel the bed dip beside me as Birdie sits, her hip touching mine. I turn my head in my hands to glance at her and her eyes catch mine. She inhales and exhales, letting breath after breath pass as we look at each other without expectation.

Then she whispers, "I'd already given up on the thought of testifying on the way here. But knowing they've dropped the charges because they don't know where I am…" Her shoulders drop suddenly with a sharp exhale. "I failed her. It's my fault they dropped the charges, and I *failed*." She stressfully rubs her palms over the tops of her thighs. "I failed…"

I drop my hands and sit up straighter, turning toward her, wrapping my arms around her, and pulling her against me. "You didn't fail. *I* failed. This is my fault, not yours."

"It's not your fault, either. You saved my life tonight, Hendrix, but it just makes me feel so broken to know that my voice will go unheard."

"It didn't go unheard with me." I pull back so I can look at her, but the glassy sheen over her eyes strikes me like lightning—the same way it struck me when she fought me so valiantly.

Her emotions are a storm that constantly swirl around me. Whether it's the passion from the way she fought for her life, the lust she felt for me after we first kissed, or the regret she feels right now, her electricity is always rumbling through the clouds of my mind, striking with a thunderous bolt when I least expect it.

"It probably feels like giving up for us to run," I say, and she agrees with a small nod, "but it's not. It would've been giving up for me if I'd done what they wanted and killed you. It would've been giving up for you if you hadn't fought me, if you'd laid there on that basement floor and let me choke the life out of you." I grab her cheeks and turn her head so our eyes meet squarely. "This—whatever this is between us—is winning. Because we aren't giving up, are we?"

Her brow furrows adorably as her eyes flick all around my face. She shakes her head subtly against my hands before her eyes drop to my lips. I run my tongue across mine before diving in to kiss her slowly, softly, deeply.

Fuck, the way she tastes me...

I drag myself away because I know that if I don't, I'll be tempted to fuck her again, and realistically, we both need to get some sleep before the night's over.

"Don't stop," she whispers as I drop my hands.

She sinks her fingers into my hair, palms covering my ears. She turns toward me, climbing up onto her knees and bending to kiss me again.

I groan, struggling against the urge to throw her down and ruin her. My hand lifts, reaching for her hair, but I ball my fist, clenching my fingers.

I lower my arm, but my hand opens as it falls, landing on her hip and squeezing. I sigh into her kiss as she leans into me.

Fuck it.

I grab her hips in both hands, lift her off her feet, and slam her down on the bed. I climb over her and settle between her legs, holding myself up on my palms as I bend down to feed her my tongue. Her knees lock around my hips, which immediately thrust forward.

Birdie moans as I rock into her, pressing, rolling my hips. Her fingers comb through my hair and scratch over my scalp, lulling me into submission to the way she makes me feel. In less than a minute, I'm gone, lost, completely absorbed in her and separate from reality... until I hear a noise at the door.

My head snaps up, turning to look at the window with

the curtains drawn before turning to the door.

Birdie's oblivious beneath me, hips moving. "Hendrix…"

I shoot up to sit back on my knees, my eyes never leaving the door. I feel her hands grapple at my abs, trying to get my attention back on her. "Hendrix?"

I bring my hand down as I bend over her slowly, covering her mouth and bringing a finger to my lips. "Shh."

My hand stays planted firmly over her lips as she rises onto her elbows. We both jump at the same time as something comes flying under the gap at the bottom of the door. I snap back to look at her.

"Quiet," I command as I pull my hand away. She nods, wide-eyed, and covers her mouth with her hand as she scoots back on the bed.

I hop off the edge, my feet landing on the carpet. Looking down, I see a piece of paper was shoved under the door. Not a full sheet, torn around the edges.

It could be from Nico, but I know in my gut it's not by the way my pulse snaps into overdrive. He wouldn't leave us in suspense like this. Immediately, my brain kicks into survival mode.

We can't get out through the door.

There's no window in the bathroom.

We can fight our way through or we can hide.

That's it. Those are our only choices.

Slowly, I bend, reaching for the paper as if my fingers are afraid it'll leap off the floor and bite them. I pluck it from the floor. There's nothing printed on the side that's face-up, so I flip it over with care, holding my breath to read it.

The moment I read the words, adrenaline flows. I drop it and spin toward Birdie, who is now on her knees on the bed. "Bathroom, run!"

And that's when it all falls apart.

She hesitates, and the part of me that needs to save her ignores the crash against the door, the way the hinges rattle as something loud and forceful slams into it from the outside.

Birdie finally moves as I rush for her, jumping off the bed. I move between her and the door, pressing my hand to the small of her back to urge her faster as she runs into the bathroom.

I bend to grab my gym bag, and as my hand wraps around the handle, there's another, and another, heavy slam against the door.

A final crash splinters the door, which startles me, causing me to stumble. I trip down to one knee, but I keep hold of the bag, dragging it with me.

My gun, my knife, her cell phone—our only defenses are in that bag. I swing my arm, sliding the bag across the threshold into the bathroom, watching it skid across the tile floor and crash at Birdie's feet. She bends to grab it and reaches her hand out toward me.

I hesitate.

I should be in there with her.

But rage lifts my chest with an insistent breath as they kick the door in behind me. I rise and step over the threshold into the bathroom. I grab the doorknob. "Lock this," I tell her as I step backward, pulling the door with me.

She says my name with fear in her eyes as I step backward, slam it shut, and turn my back on her…

And Benji fucking Baker steps over the splintered pieces of the door.

CHAPTER ELEVEN

Birdie

MY HAND IS on the knob as I prepare to open the door to whatever Hendrix is facing out there alone. I feel the pull to be with him, though I know I'm safer here, trapped behind the bathroom door.

Am I really safer?

If they want me dead, they'll kill me, locked door between us or not.

I've nearly convinced myself that I should open the door, but then I hear his voice.

The Grave Digger.

The sound is muffled, but there's no doubt in my mind because I'd know that voice anywhere—imprinted in my mind from memories that will never leave me. My fingers twist the flimsy lock on the knob, knowing that would only buy me time until they break through this door.

Maybe someone heard and they've called the police.

Who? The passed out drunk next door?

"Where is she?" Benji asks, and though their voices are

low and muffled, I can hear them clearly.

My heart picks up the pace, anxiety stemming from the sound of his voice alone. I turn to press my back against the door, slowly slipping down to sit on the cold, tiled floor.

"She's not here," Hendrix replies.

Benji chuckles. "Do you think I'm that fucking stupid? I know she's behind that door you're standing in front of. Did you tell her to lock herself in? Why even bother? You know how this ends."

"I don't know the future," Hendrix says, "but I do know that I'm not dying here tonight, and neither is she. I'm not going to let that happen."

My heart skips over an incessant beat as I oddly find some relief to hear him say that. Maybe I was still holding on to the fear that he wasn't really committed to saving me.

"You can fight if you want…" Benji says, his voice a little louder, a little closer. "You know we don't mind the entertainment. Truthfully, though, let's get on with it so we can hit the road. I need to get off-grid for a bit. Fly under the radar until all this shit with my charges and the trial dies down."

"How did you manage that one, anyway?" Hendrix asks, his tone more conversational as he asks the question I think we both already know the answer to… almost like he's stalling, buying some time.

Time isn't on our side. The devil isn't just at our doorstep—he's broken it down and let himself in. Time will only prolong the inevitable, won't it?

Nico…

I lean forward, reaching for the gym bag Hendrix threw in with me before he shut the door. I quietly pull open the zipper.

"You know, it was almost too easy getting the charges dropped." Benji's voice changes in volume, as though he's pacing. "As easy as it was to get out on bond when they first arrested me. Nobody gets out on bond for murder charges… except for me." He sounds so proud of himself. "I'm a fucking god, Hendrix, you know that. I control everything and everyone, and you and your self-righteousness aren't immune to that. Especially not when you fail to do as you're told. You fucking owed me her death."

Reaching into the bag with shaking hands, I pull out Hendrix's soiled clothes—the jeans I made him come in up against his car—and an extra hoodie. Then there's the white mask he wore when he attacked me. Next is a switchblade, which I pull out and snap open before laying it carefully— quietly—on the tile beside my hip.

Then there's his gun.

I don't know anything about guns. I don't know if it's loaded or if there's a safety. I blow out a breath, trying to ease my nerves and the tremble of my hand before I grab hold of it, carefully pulling it out of the bag.

I may have to learn to be comfortable with the idea of using this—and it may be soon. I lay the firearm beside me, taking care to aim the barrel away from me.

Finally, I spot the cell phone—*my* cell phone. I still don't know whether his friend Nico can be trusted. Maybe he set all this up and he's out there with them right now.

I have no way of knowing, but there's no one else I can call. If I call the police, and they arrive on the scene, there's no telling what they'll do. Benji might pay them off—it wouldn't surprise me. There could be a violent altercation and Hendrix could get hurt.

At the very least, he'd be arrested for my kidnapping and for Officer Hamilton's murder... and then I'd be on my own. I'd be on my own with no protection from Benji's revenge-seeking, but worse than that... I'd be without him.

I have to fight for my life... *our lives.*

I quickly scroll through my phone and find the last number dialed. I tap the screen to call. It rings three times, and when the ringing stops, it's quiet on the other end of the line.

I'm hesitant with the silence, unsure of what to say. In my pause, I realize that I no longer hear Hendrix and Benji speaking on the other side of the bathroom door.

I strain my ears to listen, then suddenly, I hear something loud and heavy slam against the door, making it rattle on its hinges, shaking me. It startles me and I yelp. At first, I think they're trying to break in, but I hear the grunts, the groans, the recognizable sound of two men fighting.

He's fighting Hendrix.

"Help," I whisper into the phone because I don't know what else to say. "They found us… Help."

The door rattles again with another thump of a body being slammed into it, startling me again, and this time I throw my hand over my mouth to muffle my scream.

"Fuck," I hear who I think is Nico on the other end of the line. "I can't help you. If they found you, I can't—"

"Please!" I shout as the fight outside the door intensifies. I think someone falls to the ground. "They're going to kill us. They'll kill Hendrix. He's your friend."

"And what the fuck am I supposed to do? Get myself killed, too? Ah, *fuck*," Nico says.

"No! I won't let you hurt her!" Hendrix shouts.

But the doorknob rattles as someone grabs hold of it from the outside. It shakes as they try to turn it, and then the pounding on the door begins. I put my foot against the side of the toilet and push back, trying to hold the door shut with my weight.

"Please," I beg Nico one last time.

Silence.

There's silence on the other end of the line, and then the call ends.

"Oh, my God." I feel tears of fear burning behind my eyes.

I throw the cell phone down, uncaring when the screen cracks as it lands on the tile. I put my other foot up on the toilet and press harder, doing everything I can to keep this door shut and give Hendrix as much time as I can to…

To do what, exactly?

To fight? To torture himself before the inevitable death that's going to meet us both?

No. I can't stop fighting now.

I glance down at the weapons beside me, easily deciding on the knife—the gun frightens me. I know I can't just leave the gun on the floor, though, obvious for them to spot as soon as they get through the door.

I grab it and put it back inside the bag, pile Hendrix's clothes on top of it, and shove the bag under the sink. Then, I pick up the knife.

My fingers curl around the wooden handle as I lift it, my hands shaking. I wrap my other palm around the fist that grips the handle, squeezing as I close my eyes and breathe in an attempt to steady myself.

Inhale, exhale.

Inhale, exhale.

My eyes snap open wide when the lock gives and the door punches against my back. I scream, but I'm not ready to give in yet. I press back, managing to push it closed again with my weight, but it only lasts a moment.

Shoving from the other side, the door creeps open, sliding me along the tile, inch by inch.

I have to gain control.

I can't let them push me anymore.

With a split-second decision, I bring my feet down,

slamming them flat to the tile. I jump up and turn as a man comes barreling into the room, stumbling forward. The unkempt man with blond hair and a beard that's too long grabs hold of the counter to right himself.

Fight.

Stab him.

Defend yourself.

I can't do this!

"Birdie!" I hear Hendrix call my name and that's all I need. That fear and desperation in the way he says it fuels me.

I let it sink inside me, heat me, trigger a rush of adrenaline that bursts through my veins. As the man stands and turns toward me, I attack. I lunge and stab the knife into his gut.

CHAPTER TWELVE
Birdie

I PULL MY arm back, stabbing him again, thrusting the blade into his stomach a second time as he doubles over my fist. He starts to fall as crimson pools and pours from his middle. I pull out the blade just before he drops, and I step back as he crumbles to his knees before me.

Oh, God. Oh, God. Oh, God…

What did I just do?

He falls sideways onto the floor, blood rushing out of him, flowing across the tile. I glance at my hand, fisted around the handle of the blade, and see the same horrible shade of red soaking my fist, dripping from it.

The bleeding man is curled into a fetal position, and his prone body blocks the door from being fully opened. Someone from the outside pushes hard against it, startling me and drawing my attention back to the urgency of my situation.

There's no time to process that I may have just killed a man. I'm still in danger—Hendrix is still in danger—and I have to act or die.

I will not die tonight.

I let out a sharp yelp when someone's head pushes through the wedged open door. I can only see half his face, but I know who it is immediately. That shaggy blond hair, the sharp cheekbones, and ugly, evil eyes.

Benji fucking Baker.

"Birdie Collins," he says with an air of annoyance, "why couldn't you just roll over and die like a good girl? I should've killed you after Nikki. I was just too excited about the thought of you living with the knowledge that you fucking failed your friend."

Something strange happens inside me. It's not just the adrenaline, it's a boiling rage that's been left on simmer since he killed her. It explodes in my chest, and I leap against reason to get after him.

Reaching over the man on the floor, I slap my palms against the door and give a forceful shove, hoping I can break his goddamn nose by slamming his head between the edge of the door and the frame at the back of his skull.

The knife slips in my bloody grip, and I feel the blade slice along my palm. My hand snaps open instinctually, letting it drop to the floor with a clang of metal hitting tile. I let up and then shove again, catching Benji off-guard enough to slam the door's edge against his face.

"Fuck!" he shouts, and internally I cheer, though I know it's nothing.

It only serves his anger.

The door flies toward me as he shoves it back with rage-fueled force. It pushes me backward and I lose my balance, stumbling as I quickly try to step back over the man on the floor.

My heel hits the edge of the bathtub behind me and my knees buckle. My shoe slips in the blood that coats the floor, and I fall backward just as I see Benji finally slip through the door.

My ass lands in the tub, my knees catching on the ledge, and feet dangling. I try to push myself out, but my bloody hands only slip and slide over the porcelain.

I have to get up.

I scramble.

Get up, Birdie!

My mind screams at me to escape, but my hands keep slipping and I can't get up.

Am I gonna die here?

Will this become a literal bloodbath?

My eyes widen as Benji steps over the man I stabbed. My breaths quicken as he reaches my feet. My pounding heart threatens to explode from my chest as he bends, a wicked sneer spread across his cheeks, and a droplet of blood dripping from one nostril. I don't even get to have a moment's satisfaction for that.

His hand shoots out and I scream as his fingers sink into my hair, gripping tight as the other grabs hold of my wrist. He yanks me up and out of the tub with a single, sharp tug, and then I'm scrambling, feet kicking and slipping over bloody tile as he jerks me around.

He gets me to the door, some man on the outside now pushing it inward, shoving the stabbed man inch by inch to force it open. Roughly, Benji turns my body, stuffing me through the narrow opening, my curves scraping along the wooden frame.

As I burst forth into the room, tripping over my feet before quickly righting myself, I take in the sight of horror.

Hendrix is on the floor, arms jerked behind him and secured. His back rests against the side of the bed, his bloodied and bruised face tilting toward his shoulder. He looks beaten and tired, though the fire still burns through his heaving chest.

A man stands in front of him, aiming a gun at his head, and another man guards the door.

Hendrix's eyes lift to meet mine with gentleness and fear, but quickly looking beyond me, flicking to Benji at my back, the gentleness switches to pure hatred.

I run for Hendrix—I have no control over my reaction— but I don't get far.

Benji's hand is in my hair at the base of my skull, and he jerks me back. My hands shoot up to grab his—a natural reaction to try to relieve the tension and pain of his pulling. His other hand comes around my waist and I glance down at it as I feel his body mold to my backside.

Looking down was a mistake…

He's holding the bloody blade I dropped, running the flat edge across my shirt. I suck in my stomach with a sharp breath, panic dripping through my insides.

"I'll fucking kill you," Hendrix says through gritted teeth, and I see blood smeared across them. His eyes are wide and fixed on Benji. "Hurt her and I'll fucking *end* you." His tone reflects a cold, quiet fury.

"This is cute, really," Benji replies. "You've got your own little tragic one-night stand romance going on here, don't you?"

I hold my breath as he wipes the blade down the side of my hip.

"I didn't plan on having any fun tonight… but you know I live for the drama, X," he says to Hendrix. "The hit-turned-kidnapping, my charges being dropped at the eleventh hour, this little cat-and-mouse game trying to find you two… and now this…" He points the tip of the blade toward Hendrix, then toward my chest, causing me to gasp. "You two seem to have some sort of thing going on between you. It makes you think, you know? What's really important in life?" He brings his face in close, his mouth moving against my ear. "I'm a romantic at heart, Birdie. I really am. It's what Nikki was drawn to when I met her, you know?"

My whole body jerks with the urge to hurt him at the mention of her name.

"It's just that I get bored easily. And people are the

best form of entertainment, aren't they? It's why I created numb. Bring chaos to the masses. Well, not chaos exactly… It just really brings them down to that maddening level of melancholy, that level that forces them to face just how meaningless their lives really are. Some bounce back from it with a new lease on life—grab it by the balls, you know? But the others are my favorites… the ones so lost in the pointlessness of life that all they can think about is the sweet relief of death. Those are the ones who make the best fucking headlines."

Benji releases me all at once, pushing me forward unexpectedly, and I fall onto my hands and knees. Immediately, I start crawling, moving toward the bed to get to Hendrix.

"Anyway, I digress," Benji says just as I reach him. "I suggest we take this to a more secure location as I'd like to take my time dragging this out." He smiles and it's filled with vileness. "Take them to the car."

CHAPTER THIRTEEN
Hendrix

THEY SHOVE HER into the trunk of the car before forcing me in after. I fought them as much as I could, using my shoulders to jab and feet to kick since that's all I could really do with my hands still bound behind my back. My body stills as the trunk slams shut, casting us in darkness.

We're close.

I can feel Birdie's breath on my bruised cheek.

"Are you hurt? Did he cut you?" I whisper quickly.

"No, I… Well, I cut my hand a little, but it wasn't him. I'm okay."

"Fuck, angel, I'm so sorry—"

"This isn't your fault."

"Did you call him?" I shift my body, bending and bumping my knees against her as I maneuver to wiggle my arms down past my ass.

"What?"

"Nico, did you call him?"

Once my arms are down, I shift again, struggling to

pull my legs through and get my arms in front of me. The engine starts and the car moves forward, jostling us against each other in the trunk.

"Oh, God. Where are they taking us?" Panic rises in her voice.

"Did you call Nico?" I repeat.

"I… Yes, I called him, but he said he couldn't help us. He said if they found us, then it's already too late. Then we got cut off… or maybe he hung up. I can't remember."

"But you spoke with him? And you're sure it was his voice? Did he sound surprised they'd found us?"

"Yes, I'm sure it was him. I guess he sounded shocked… scared… but he made it clear he couldn't help us, Hendrix, so I don't know why that matters."

"Hope is why it matters. He might come through."

"What are you *talking* about?"

The pitch in her voice rises, her panic pulsing from her in anxious waves. Twice in a trunk in the same goddamn night, and I feel like shit for what I did to her. But there's no time to think about that now. I just have to get us out of this.

I promised I'd save her, and I'm going to.

I shift my body forward, scooting against her, and in the dark, I search for her lips with mine, brushing across her cheek before finding them. I steal a kiss from her. Slipping my tongue between her lips, I sink deeply, trying to coax the strength from her with the passion that lives inside her soul and makes her fight.

I force myself to pull away. "Can you get your hands in front of you?"

"Yeah, I think so."

I feel her moving, wriggling and twisting to get her arms—which they bound behind her back—in front of her body.

I know when they're clear because I feel her fingers touch my bare chest, warming me with determination.

"I'm gonna get the trunk open and I need you to be ready, okay?"

"Ready for what?"

"When they slow, we're gonna jump out."

"*What?*"

I roll over to face the other way, feeling her fingers sweep across my skin as I turn my back to her. Her fingers don't leave me, palms pressing to my back as I search with my hands for a trunk release that might not even be there.

"We can't jump out," she says frantically. "They'll just stop the car and chase after us anyway, if we haven't broken a leg in the process."

"It's a chance we have to take. It'll be worse than broken bones if they get us back to Benji's place. He'll torture us until we're begging for death."

"How do you even know that?"

"People talk, Birdie. I told you he's a sick, sadistic motherfucker."

My fingers grope along the carpeted interior, but I'm

coming up short. If there were a trunk release here, they've removed it.

"Fuck!" I angrily punch my fists against the trunk lid.

"What is it?" she asks.

"I can't find a goddamn trunk release."

"What are we gonna do?"

I roll onto my back, closing my eyes and taking a few steadying breaths.

There has to be a way out of this.

Something you haven't thought of yet.

Her voice is a whisper that I almost don't hear. "Is this it for us?"

My heart drops into my gut.

This can't be it for us.

It just can't be.

I just fucking found her, and it doesn't matter how anymore. We were meant to find each other, I *know* it. And if we were meant to find each other, then we were meant for more than just tonight, more than this, more than torture and a slow, painful death.

I roll toward her again, wrapping my palms around her small hands. "No. This isn't it for us because we're gonna fight like hell. You're gonna fight them the same way you fought me, okay? You're not gonna stop until you break free, because that's our only option. You weren't meant to die tonight, and neither was I."

"I need more time with you," she murmurs, her lips

grazing my knuckles. "That's stupid because I just met you… but I can't lose you."

"You won't. I swear, Birdie, you won't."

The car slams to a tire-screeching halt, a red glow from the brake lights at my back creeping in around us. My body rolls into hers as she's pushed forcefully toward the front of the car. When the car stops entirely, momentum releasing, we're thrown back and she rolls into me.

Everything stops… then starts again all at once.

Car doors open.

Shouts are heard.

"Who the fuck are you?" someone nearby hollers. "Get back in your fucking car or I'm gonna blow your head off."

What the fuck?

"Get back!"

Gunfire erupts, the first shot fired toward us, and I know this because we hear the bullet skip across the metal shell of the car somewhere near our feet.

Birdie yelps and I lift my hands, threading her head between my arms and looping them around her shoulders. I roll toward her, pushing her back, covering her body with mine to block the next missed shot that could come ripping through the metal.

"Stay still," I tell her as she flinches against each gunshot being fired outside the car.

"What's happening?"

"I don't know. Just stay under me and don't move."

People are going down. I hear shots and protests, orders yelled. I hear the distinctive sound of Benji scream right after a *pop*, "Get me out of here!"

We hear a couple of car doors slam, then the screech of tires as a car—probably the one Benji was in behind us—peels off into the night. The gunfire fades into silence after what could've been seconds or minutes, I don't really know.

Then nothing but eerie, unsettling silence.

Who the fuck did they run into?

Police?

An enemy?

How the fuck are we getting out of this?

When I feel confident that the gunfire has ceased, I lift my arms and roll away from her, turning to face the trunk.

The car engine cuts off.

I ball my hands into fists, ready to strike if someone opens it… and I know someone is about to because I hear movement and the jingling of keys.

"Oh, God," Birdie mutters at my back.

The latch releases with a startling snap and the trunk pops open. Standing with a black leather-gloved hand gripping the lid is a man dressed in black, wearing the familiar white mask of the Senseless—the same mask I wore earlier tonight.

I'm just about to whip my feet around, hoping to kick him in the gut and knock him backward… but then he says, "Jesus, X. I thought you were fucked."

Fucking Nico.

He pulls down his hood, revealing his familiar undercut—black hair where it's buzzed on the sides, with longer tufts of messily styled shamrock-green on top. He lifts his mask and tosses it to the ground before leaning over us, pulling a switchblade from his back pocket.

I let out a sigh of relief as I hold out my hands to him. He slices through the cable tie, and I climb out of the trunk, taking the blade from him.

"It's okay," I tell Birdie, leaning over the edge to cut her cable tie free.

She looks between us as I fold the blade and hand it back to Nico, then hold my hand out for her. She has some hesitation as she reaches her hand out for me.

I suppose I'd be concerned if she didn't show any apprehension, given all the twists and turns of tonight. But eventually, she takes my hand and lets me help her climb out.

As soon as her feet land on pavement, I wrap my arms around her and tug her into my embrace. I kiss the side of her head before grabbing hold of her shoulders and gently pushing back.

I look down at her face and see how her attention is fixed on Nico, understandably wary. "I thought you couldn't help us," she says with an air of agitation.

"I couldn't," Nico replies. "I *shouldn't* have. I'm as fucked as you two are now when they figure out it was me."

I turn toward him, and we clap hands before pulling it in for a hug. "Fuck, man, I thought you were dead."

I glance around him to see a bloodied corpse lying on the ground beside the driver's side door. "Thanks to you, we're not."

"I nicked Benji, bro," Nico says, running a hand through his green hair. "I got both the guys driving this car, but the other two pulled Benji into the SUV following you and they sped off. Shit, if they find out it was me—"

"You'll cover it up. It's what you do best. If anyone can hide this from them, it's you."

Nico is an expert in finding people—and has equal expertise in hiding Senseless criminals and crimes from the police. If he can cover up Senseless crimes, he sure as fuck can keep this under wraps. Still, his anxiety is understandable. If Benji finds out he did this…

"Come on," Nico says. "We need to get the fuck out of here."

Barefoot and shirtless, I grab Birdie's hand and we take off after Nico, running to a black pickup truck—a vehicle that definitely isn't his—that's stopped in the middle of the dark, empty road before us.

Nico jumps into the driver's seat as I open the passenger door for Birdie, helping her step up into the truck before climbing in after her. We settle into the bench seat, and I wrap my arm around her shoulders, pulling her close against my side as Nico peels off into the night.

I sense her unease seated beside Nico, particularly in the way she presses her hip so closely to mine.

"You said you couldn't help us," she says again with her head turned, looking at him squarely.

"Yeah, well… I changed my mind."

"Why?"

"I don't know. Things sounded pretty fucking dramatic on your end, doll. I guess I'm a bit soft-hearted these days… even if it is gonna get me killed."

"It's not gonna get you killed," I tell him. "They'll never figure it out."

"Never say never, X. Anything's possible." Nico glances over, his eyes flickering between the both of us. "I guess you two figured that out tonight, huh?"

Birdie and I look at each other at the same moment. "Yeah, you could say that."

A hint of a smile flares at the corners of her lips, her shoulders slowly releasing some tension.

"Open that," Nico says, his finger lifting from the steering wheel, pointing toward the glove box in front of me. "I didn't have time to make your passports since blondie called me to come in a little early, so you can't leave the country. But I've got licenses, social security cards, and documents in there for both of you." He looks over at us, and I see humor touch his eyes as he chuckles. "Made a marriage certificate, too… I thought it'd be funny, but maybe that'll work out in your favor."

"Moving a little fast, aren't we?" Birdie reaches forward, popping open the glove box. She retrieves a manilla envelope, lifts the flap, and glances at the documents inside it.

"Technically, you should be dead," Nico says. "So, I say grab life by the balls and live fast because tomorrow is promised to no one, especially you two."

"Everything's legit?" I ask. "We can disappear with this?"

"That's the goal. I suggest low-key living. Don't draw attention to yourselves. Maybe change your hair. Find jobs you wouldn't normally choose. I've got a car for you. Sell it as soon as you can and use the cash to buy another one.

"Things should quiet down on you two in a year or so. Grave Digger holds grudges, but who knows…? Maybe I got lucky and nicked an artery and he's bleeding out as we speak." He runs a nervous hand through his bright green hair.

I've never seen Nico this way—so anxious and unsettled. It's reasonable panic because he's just made an enemy out of Benji Baker. I fucking hope he's got a good plan to cover his tracks because he'll meet a horrible death if they find out it was him. He may have just fucked himself over to save our lives.

"We can't ever repay you for this, Nico."

"No, you can't," he says with a tight smile. "And don't try. We can't be in contact anymore. Don't come back here, don't call—not me, not your friends, not your family. That bloodbath we just left behind…? The Senseless won't want that getting out. Benji won't want the media getting wind of the fact that he's injured… that some rando wearing a mask from his own crew took out two of his men. He'll have Merrick handle it, and he's gonna want me to spin a story about it.

"I'm gonna tell him to name you as the people who died, okay? Senseless are gonna take credit for your deaths to send a message, and you have to let it be. That's the best thing that could happen to you in this shit—the world thinking you're dead. And I'll just have to hope I'll be as good at covering my own damn tracks as I am at covering everyone else's."

"God, thank you," Birdie says softly. "Really, thank you. You don't know me and you saved me. You saved us both."

"Don't mention it, doll. We're all just trying to survive this Senseless shit."

Birdie settles into my hold as Nico drives us along the dark path.

This was all set into motion long before tonight.

This path was set for us before we could choose it because it was set by the stars. The way that I find comfort and peace through such ardent chaos, simply from the heat of her at my side is beyond logic.

She and I were meant to find each other, and though we found each other darkly, on the bleakest of nights, we have the electricity from our lightning strike meeting to brighten our path.

CHAPTER FOURTEEN

Birdie

THE RED DYE drips down my back as I stand in the shower, head tilted beneath the spray. My eyes are shut as I rinse the color from my hair. I tried brown before, but it only looked like a darker, warmer shade of my natural color, and I felt like I looked too much like the old me.

Change is just a part of my life now. We've been hopping from one motel to the next on our little tour of small towns where people go to hide from the world.

X thinks we can settle soon, and I agree. But soon isn't now, so we're still on the go, restless when we stay in one place for too long.

We keep our eyes on the news. Someone—Nico, we assume—had covered up the shooting on the dark road where he picked us up that night, just like Nico had told us. Media reported that X and I were found dead on that stretch of highway where Nico had saved our lives.

The Senseless are after Nico now—I should say, they're

after the unknown masked man who put a bullet in the Grave Digger.

I don't think Benji's dead and neither does X. Publicly, there's speculation over his lack of presence in Senseless affairs. A new name is circulating through people associated with the Senseless—Merrick, a man Hendrix was associated with previously. Some think Benji's dead and that Merrick rules now, but I just know in my gut that's not the case.

I know Benji's still alive… it wouldn't be that easy to get rid of him.

I blow out a breath as my hands slip down my hair. I open my eyes and drop my head, turning to reach for the shampoo from the ledge. I spot the burgundy dye coating the white tub beneath my feet, and my heart stops with a flash vision.

Suddenly, I'm back in that motel room the night they found us, when Benji broke into the bathroom and I slipped in blood, falling back into the tub. Panic rises to overwhelm me and I lower myself to my knees as faintness makes my head feel light.

My head drops down as my breaths quicken, and I'm only closer to the red dye that mixes with the running water, swirling around my feet.

Benji's face flashes before my eyes—the way he came for me as I sat stuck in that tub, my bloodied hand slipping against it as I tried to push myself up.

"X," I manage to get out as the anxiety builds.

Thank God he's already in the bathroom brushing his teeth because I don't know if I could yell loud enough for him to hear me, and I *need* him. He's the only thing that gets me through these stress flashes of panic from that traumatic fucking night.

"Yeah," he mumbles, and I hear him turn the faucet on and spit.

"Help," I whisper.

The shower curtain opens to reveal him on the other side, shirtless in his black boxer briefs, concern etched across his stubbled face. "What's wrong, angel?"

He doesn't wait for me to answer as he steps over the ledge, climbing into the tub with me with his underwear still on.

"The red…" I say through intentional deep breaths, "it looks like blood in the tub and I had a stupid flashback."

"You're safe," he tells me, reaching out to pry my fingers from their death grip on the ledge, scooting in close on his knees in front of me. "We're safe. No one's going to hurt you."

I blow out a breath. "We're safe."

His knuckles brush beneath my chin, giving a little nudge of encouragement for me to lift my head. Our eyes meet, and I hold on fiercely to his gaze—the only thing that can center me as I fight through the anxiety.

He keeps my chin tilted up, angling my head beneath the water as his other hand comes up to run through my hair.

He strokes my head, but he also combs his fingers through, finishing the task for me and rinsing out the remaining dye.

The way his eyes hold mine while he cares for me so gently helps me concede to the panic, let it rise to its peak, knowing I'm safe here with him. The anxiety quickly crests, my chest rising and falling sharply as tears burn behind my eyes, but he continues, kindly rinsing my hair and holding my gaze to comfort me.

"Almost done," he says, and though he could mean with the rinsing, I know he means the panic—he's gotten me through enough of these episodes over the last month that he knows how they flow better than I do.

Sure enough, I can feel it fading—not disappearing entirely, but lessening enough that my strength has space to creep back in.

"Look down," he says, and I do. "No more red. The water's clear. You're here with me, not back there with him."

I nod as he touches my cheek, his thumb brushing across my lip.

"I'm safe."

"You're safe," he gives me a small smile, then lets out his own long-held breath.

I know my anxiety attacks are as stressful on him as they are on me. He slips his arms around me and pulls me close, our bodies aligned as I rise up on my knees to meet him. I cling to him as he holds me, craving the dopamine rush I get from the way he cares for me.

"Come here," he says, turning me around.

He moves us to sit on the opposite end of the tub, sliding me back to settle between his legs. I lean back against his strong chest and let my head fall onto his shoulder. He wraps his arms around me, holding me sweetly.

A few quiet breathing moments pass.

"Maybe red was a bad idea," I chuckle.

His hand strokes down my hair. "It looks good on you."

I close my eyes to savor the feeling of his stroking hand. "You said that about the brown dye, too."

"You look perfect in any color, angel."

I sigh, sinking in his hold, my shoulders finally relax as his hand drops, and he slowly strokes my arm.

"I'm sorry," I tell him. "I don't know how you put up with me."

"Put up with you? Fuck, no. It's a privilege to be the only man who gets to see all of you."

"What do you mean?"

"You know what I mean. I see the best and the worst. I get you from every angle. I see every curve and blind spot in your mind because you let yourself break in front of me. You've given me your vulnerability—something you never owed to me, but you gave it anyway. I'm the luckiest fucking man alive because I know every inch of you, angel… body and soul."

My eyes drift shut, lulled by the deepness of his tone and the honesty in his words. The way his stroking fingers add pressure as they move up and down my arm makes my skin prickle with goosebumps.

My voice is finally calm when I speak, "Have I told you yet today that I'm gonna fall in love with you?"

"Not today…" I hear his smile. "You told me yesterday."

"I'm gonna fall in love with you."

He falls silent, which is not unusual when I tell him that. It doesn't worry me or make me feel uncomfortable. We've only known each other for a month, and our paths were forced to cross in the worst of ways. His silence doesn't make me concerned, it just… is.

His fingers leave my arm and I briefly mourn the loss of them before they come up to pull my wet hair back and tuck it behind my ear. His face comes in close, his lips brushing the shell of my ear, his warm breath on my skin sending a current of pleasure down the side of my neck.

"Go ahead and fall in love with me, angel," he whispers. "Because I'm already in love with you."

My head turns sharply so I can look at his face over my shoulder. His dark eyes are hooded beneath the line of his eyebrows, watching me with all the seriousness in the world. My eyes roam his face as we watch each other, taking in every feature, every tick in his expression as his breaths deepen, and his chest rises and falls against my back.

"Kiss me—"

I hardly get the words out before his lips land on mine, kissing me with frantic calmness, trying to be easy with me after my panic, though I can feel the need for connection humming from his touch. I part my lips, encouraging the hectic rush.

His tongue circles mine, licking and swirling with intent, making me moan. Our kiss breaks when I whimper at the touch of his hand covering my breast, fingers teasing and playing on my skin.

"I'm gonna make you come, angel," he says as steam from the shower swirls around us. He rubs his nose across my cheek. "You're gonna let me finger-fuck you to bliss, because you're mine, aren't you?"

"Yes," I breathe out slowly as one hand creeps down my belly, teasing over my curls. "Please."

His fingers dip as I spread my legs for him, brushing lightly over my folds and teasing across my clit. I press my hands down into his thighs as he plays, his light touch teasing and intoxicating.

My eyes are shut as he nuzzles and kisses my neck, my jaw, my cheek. I'm enveloped in heat from every angle, from the warm water splashing my ankles to his hard body behind me to his heated breath blowing over my skin.

He brings two fingers back and presses in against my clit, making me stiffen as he pulses pressure against the spot, causing me to swell and ache pleasantly.

"I love making you come." He kisses beneath my jaw, moving down my neck. "I'll never get tired of the way it makes me feel to watch you squirm under my hand."

Squirming is the right word for the way he makes my body shift. He gives me pleasure so intensely that it makes me equally want to move away *and* move into it, struggling with the overwhelming sensation and whether I need more or less.

Of course, I always need more.

When he's sufficiently tortured my clit with pulsing pressure and stroking circles, his fingers slip down and press slightly into my opening. My hands clench around his muscular thighs, trying to keep myself upright, though my body slips along the tub.

He dips his fingers in deep, twisting his hand as he groans at my back. He uses the way his fingers are sunk inside to grip me, dragging my slipping body back to him, his hand like a hook hoisting me back. The pain and force of it causes such aching, blissful stretching inside me that I moan and whimper.

"Oh, my God…"

I feel the aggressive switch flip inside him, the way passion takes hold of him as he draws out his fingers and shoves them in again, deeply.

We both like when he's just a little rough.

"Three," his tone has turned gruff and insistent, which switches me on and coils tight in my belly, "Can you take three fingers, angel? I want to stretch you so wide it hurts." He licks behind my ear, and I'm lost entirely to the world around us.

"Yes, do it."

His hand turns as he wedges a third finger inside me, his thumb and pinky on the outside pressing into my flesh as he punches the other three digits in and out, twisting and thrusting and making it hurt so good.

Each time he pulls out before thrusting back in, my body slips lower down the tub, away from him. I try to hold myself up on his legs, but he has me so consumed with painful lust that I can't, and I just keep slipping.

He pumps in and out of me until I'm panting and twitching, my clit throbbing to be touched again. But then he pulls his fingers out, leaving me empty. In a snap, his ass slides forward toward my slipping form, and he sits up straight behind me. He reaches over me and flips off the shower so the water flows heavily through the low faucet instead.

He grips my shoulders, pushing me down as he moves us forward, toward the drain. "Feet on the wall," he commands.

I'm not really sure what's happening here.

"Feet. Up," he says again while reaching around to grab my knees and lifting.

I raise my legs at his insistence, putting my feet flat on the tile wall on either side of the faucet. His hands fall to my hips, and he shoves me even further down until I'm lying back with my head on his thigh.

His palms slip slowly down my body, caressing over

my breasts, fingers playing with my nipples. They move down my stomach, massaging up my thighs and back down again until they land between my legs. He toys with my pussy, rubbing all over—between the lips, exploring every untouched part of me.

And then his fingers spread me open, exposing my clit, and I feel the splash of warm water from the running faucet.

"Move your ass down, get under the water, angel." He holds me open as I adjust my hips, sinking fully beneath the flow until the force of it is raining down on my clit.

"X," I moan as I grip his ankles.

The weight of the water is heavy as it falls, pounding down on my pussy.

He groans behind me, moving one hand to keep me spread open with two fingers forming a 'V'. He reaches lower with his other hand to play, rubbing along my slit, dipping a finger inside me, drawing back to rub over my clit.

That hand continues to roam and play as pressure builds, my eyes floating shut and head rolling over his leg.

He hisses as my legs start to twitch, as my muscles contract against the overwhelming pleasure pounding on my clit. "Come on, angel, come for me. Come hard. Let this be the only memory you have of being helpless in a bathtub."

"Say it again," I breathe. "Tell me you love me."

I open my eyes to find him looking down at me, his gaze skimming over my body before landing on my eyes.

"I love you. I want you." He takes in a sharp breath as he shudders. "You're fucking mine."

My climax hits me spectacularly with the way he claims me, pulsing through my clit. My back arches, my legs shake, my hips raise to unashamedly fuck the stream of water and draw out this heavy, insistent orgasm.

I pant through the intensity as it peaks then plummets, legs still shaking. He reaches beneath my arms and drags me back sharply. Once I'm sitting up, I turn to face him, eager to return the favor.

I get up onto my knees, feeling weak and wobbly from the drop of such strong pleasure. My thighs are twitching, my whole body trembling with sensitivity.

I grab hold of the edge of the tub as I sit back on my heels, waiting as he shoves the elastic of his underwear down and frees his cock before slipping the boxer briefs down his thighs.

"I want that," I tell him, biting my lip as I look down at it.

"I know you do."

I climb onto his lap, slipping my legs around his waist as I brace my arms against the edges. I'm eager to be filled, quickly wiggling my hips until I feel my wetness slide across his hard length. His hand touches my cheek and his fingers tangle into my hair, pulling me closer to kiss me with all the passion of a man in love.

He's in love with me.

I find the tip of his cock as my hips wriggle, and he slides easily inside me. I cross my ankles around his back, letting go of the tub edges to wrap myself fully around him and hold on tight. I hug him close as I move my hips with a rolling thrust, feeling him along every ridge inside me.

He lets me move slowly, sensually, building the tension between us simultaneously as our breath mingles.

His hand strokes down my head. "You make me feel so good, angel."

"You make me feel better, X. You make me feel everything."

He sighs as I fuck him slowly, his embrace tightening, face nuzzling into my neck to kiss and lick. "Tell me again that you're gonna fall for me one day."

I sink my fingers into his hair at the base of his skull, gripping tight and jerking his head back to force him to look at me.

"You know I lied when I told you that before."

His eyes narrow as he watches me, waiting for me to go on.

"I was just afraid to scare you off with the truth."

"Tell me the truth."

"You know I've already fallen for you." I massage his scalp. "I'm in too deep to ever dig my way out."

He watches me for beats as I continue to move, my rolling hips gradually picking up a pace that makes him grit his teeth and hiss.

His hand falls to grip the back of my neck, pulling me closer so our foreheads meet, his eyes burrowing deeply into mine. "You mean it?"

"I love you, X. I'm completely fucking in love with you—"

His kiss cuts me off, cracking me open, splintering me down the center of my soul to make room for him to pass through.

No, not to pass through… to *merge*.

Our souls merge as he kisses me with confession, with a silent oath that we've senselessly fallen for each other.

Our shared love builds passion and grows tension. Our lips stay locked as we fuck, grinding through a slow-building ache that takes forever and no time at all to reach a breaking point.

When we come, we come together—just as we'll be for the rest of our lives.

He and I were meant to be—our fates intertwined. It all could've ended that night we met, but we chose a different destiny instead. We could leave each other and build new lives separately on our own. Maybe that would make it harder for the Senseless to find us when they someday decide we're a grudge they can no longer ignore, but we choose to be together.

"I choose you," I say as I hug him tight. "Always."

"We choose each other," he replies.

And I know we always will.

CONNECT WITH BRYNN

Website
brynnford.com

Goodreads
goodreads.com/brynnfordauthor

BookBub
bookbub.com/profile/brynn-ford

Instagram
@brynnfordauthor
instagram.com/brynnfordauthor

TikTok
@brynnfordauthor
tiktok.com/@brynnfordauthor

Facebook Page
facebook.com/brynnfordauthor

Brynn's Daring Darlings
(Facebook Group)
bit.ly/brynnsdarlings

BRYNN'S BOOKS

THE FOUR FAMILIES TRILOGY
Counts of Eight
Dance with Death
Pas de Trois

THE FOUR FAMILIES SPIN-OFF
King of Masters

EMBER GLEN
Spark of Madness
Blaze of Misery
Embers of Mercy

SENSELESS
(Novellas)
Unheard
Unseen

STANDALONES
Jagged Line Paradise
Sugar Wood

ABOUT THE AUTHOR

Brynn Ford is a USA Today Bestselling Author of dark romance for daring readers. She writes emotionally heavy love stories that will twist your soul and shatter your heart before pulling you back together with a hopeful happily-ever-after.

Brynn's books are dark, sometimes disturbing, and often overwhelming. But they're always brightened by an insistent, spicy romance that will live rent-free in your head long after you've turned the final page.

When Brynn isn't obsessively writing, you may find her binge-watching favorite shows while eating far too much junk food or fanatically reading, always seeking to lose herself in the emotional roller coaster of a damn good story. She's a firm believer that her characters continue to live outside the pages in the minds of her readers. Stories don't end just because there aren't any more pages to turn.

9 781955 349130